# Kissing
## THE
# RIVAL

NEW YORK TIMES BESTSELLING AUTHOR
# KAYLEE RYAN

Cover Design: Book Cover Boutique
Cover Photography: Wander Aguair
Editing: Hot Tree Editing
Proofreading: Deaton Author Services,
Jo Thompson, Jess Hodge
Paperback Formatting: Integrity Formatting

# THE *Kissing* GAMES

*There are five books in the series.*

*Authors include:*
*Molly McLain, Kaylee Ryan,*
*C.A. Harms, Lacey Black, and Evan Grace.*

*All books can be read as standalone novels,*
*and can be read in any order.*

# Prologue

 *Charlotte*

### Clemson University, Freshman Year

WALKING INTO THE LARGE AUDITORIUM, I scan the room. There are students milling around everywhere and the sounds of their voices echo throughout the room. My knees are shaking and my palms are wet from sweat. I don't know that I've ever been this nervous. I don't know a single person at this university and I have more problems in my life than a math test, but I'm here, and I'm determined to see this through.

I *have* to see this through.

Leaving home and saying goodbye to my little sister was one of the hardest things I've ever had to do. I've questioned my decision more times than I can count, but at the end of the day, I know this is what's best. She's in good hands with Aunt Miranda. She might not be the most loving of parental figures, but she's what we have, and I'll check in with Audrey daily. She'll barely know I'm not there.

Finding a seat in the back, I plop down, setting my backpack with all my essentials at my feet. I've never been to one of the college freshman orientations. I don't know if I need something while here, and I don't want to be *that* girl—the shy one with no friends to sit with and who doesn't have what she needs.

But I'm here nonetheless.

As I glance at my wrist, pain pierces my chest when I see my dad's watch. He wasn't wearing it the night of the accident. It's the first thing I noticed when I went into my parents' room. I asked Audrey if she wanted it, but she said no. It's far too large for my tiny wrist, but I can't seem to go a day without wearing it. Aunt Miranda tells me it will get easier—that time heals all wounds—but I'm pretty sure she's mistaken. I don't know that any amount of time will fill the hole of the loss of my parents.

Reaching into my backpack for my phone to text my sister, I hear a deep "Hey" next to me. Turning, I see a guy with dark brown hair, the most amazing brown eyes I've ever seen, and a smile that I'm sure has the ladies lining up for his attention.

"Hi." I tuck my hair behind my ear and quickly type out a message to my little sister.

**Me:** What are you up to?

**Audrey:** I'm in business ethics class.

**Me:** Why are you replying if you're in class?

**Audrey:** Why are you texting me when you know I'm in class?

She has a point.

"I'm Spencer," the hot guy says. I look over, and he offers me a grin and his hand. I take it.

"Charlotte." I used to hate my full name, only my parents used it, but now that they're gone, I long to hear them say it just one more time.

"Nice to meet you, Charlotte."

"You too," I say, going back to my phone.

THE *Kissing* GAMES

**Me:** Call me when you get out of school, and we'll catch up.

**Audrey:** You've been gone for three days, Charlie. There isn't much to catch up on.

**Me:** I miss you.

I can practically see her rolling her eyes at me.

**Audrey:** I miss you too. I'll call you later. Aren't you supposed to be in orientation?

I send her a quick picture of the auditorium.

**Me:** I'm here. Just waiting for it to start.

**Audrey:** You've got this, big sister.

**Me:** We've got this.

A man steps up to the podium, raises his hand, and the room starts to quiet down.

**Me:** Starting. Gotta go.

I slide my phone back into the front pocket of my bag and keep my eyes on the man front and center.

"Boyfriend?" Spencer asks from his seat next to me.

I turn my head just slightly to look at him. "What?"

He nods to where I just shoved my phone back in my bag. "Texting your boyfriend?"

"No."

"Husband?"

This time I turn and give him my full attention. "Do I look like I'm married?" My voice comes out a little harsher than I intended. That's been my normal stance since we lost our parents three short months ago. I don't mean to come off short, but I'm just so damn angry, I don't know how to deal with it. I hate that I had to leave my sister with our aunt, and I hate the unknown.

"I don't know. A beautiful girl like you"—Spencer shrugs—"it wouldn't surprise me if someone decided to put a ring on it."

I raise my left hand and wiggle my fingers. "Nope." Before he can respond, the president of the university begins his welcome speech. The room falls silent as we all hang on to his every word. An hour later, we're finally dismissed, and I'm still riddled with anxiety about the unknown.

"Hey, Charlotte, want to grab a coffee?" Spencer asks. He shoves his hands into his pockets and rocks back on his feet. I notice a tattoo that peeks out from beneath his Clemson T-shirt.

"I can't."

"How about we exchange numbers, and we can meet up later? Or another time?" he offers.

"Yo, Spence, we're going to head to the quad. You coming?" another guy calls out.

I follow the voice and see a guy with brown hair sitting a few rows down from us. He's looking between Spencer and me, wearing a smirk.

"That's my roommate, Lincoln," he explains. "What do you say?" Spencer asks, pulling my attention back to him.

"I don't think so. It was nice meeting you." Standing, I grab my backpack and wait patiently for him to move out of the row so that I can follow him.

"Come on, don't be like that," he says as a group of girls pass, waving hi, and calling out his name.

"Looks like you don't need me," I tell him, nodding to the small group that just passed, giggling and looking back at him over their shoulders.

"You jealous?"

"Nope. Just not interested." I square my shoulders and peer up at him. I'm tall at five foot eight, but I still have to look up to him. My guess is he's at least six foot two. "If you'll excuse me." I make myself as small as I can as I step around him and rush down the aisle and down the steps out of the auditorium.

THE *Kissing* GAMES

Three months ago, I would have jumped at the chance to have coffee with him, and I might have even been the one to suggest that we exchange numbers, but I'm no longer that person. I no longer live the life of a carefree eighteen-year-old. I have to keep my eye on the prize, and the prize is my education and my scholarship. If I lose it, I lose college. I don't want to take out loans and be in debt. I feel bad enough that we had to sell the house we grew up in to pay off the mortgage. I don't have my parents to rely on for help. I have me and my sixteen-year-old little sister, who I will never and would never pass this burden onto.

I need to stay focused. I don't have time for distractions or relationships. When I graduate, when I know that I have secured my future, there will be time for that.

Right now, there is just too much at stake.

 *Spencer*

### *Clemson University, Senior Year*

PROFESSOR ELLIOTT STANDS AT THE front of the lecture hall with his glasses perched on the end of his nose. This is my second economics class with him, and every single day I've wanted to just step up next to him and push the damn things up on his face.

"I have your midterms." He raises a stack of papers in the air. "As you know, we have two students competing for the highest grade in this class." His eyes flash from me to Charlotte, who's sitting in the row in front of me. "I'm happy to say that we have a new leader."

A slow smile tilts my lips. Everyone knows that Charlotte had the highest GPA in this class, and they also know that I am right behind her. That could only mean that I stole the top spot from miss perfect.

It's a shame she's so closed off and thinks she's better than everyone else. She's a fucking knockout. I can still remember the first day I laid eyes on her. Lincoln, my best friend and roommate, and I were headed to freshman orientation. We were both pumped. When I walked into the room and saw her, I knew I had to meet her. I needed to know her name and hear the sound of her voice. Her long, auburn hair stood out among every other woman in the room, and when I got closer, I saw her eyes. A bright blue I'd never seen before but a color I still manage to see in my dreams.

Yeah, I've got a thing for her. Not because I'm in love with her or anything. She's sexy as fuck. Too bad she's also got a stick up her ass and has become my rival.

She shot me down instantly. She didn't flirt or act coy. She truly wasn't interested. At least, that's what I thought. We've had several classes together over the years, and she's remained closed off, distant, and, well, stuck up. It's not even her beauty that makes her that way. She's not all "I'm sexy, and I know it." No, Charlotte is just one of those people who thrives on being the best. She doesn't flaunt it, but I know she gets off on beating me. That's why I can't resist moving seats so that I can lean over and flaunt my win.

"Whatcha got there, Charlie?" That's something else. I called her Charlie at the beginning of our sophomore year, and she reprimanded me, reminding me her name was Charlotte. I've called her Charlie ever since.

Sure, it's petty, but that's how we are with one another.

Hell, if I didn't know better, I'd say it's been four very long years of foreplay.

She turns in her seat and glares at me. "What did you get?" She holds up her paper, and I can see the ninety-eight written at the top in bold red sharpie.

My grin widens. I hold up my paper so she can see, and she huffs out a breath when she notices my bright red ninety-nine displayed the same way.

"One freaking point," she mutters.

"Why don't you give me your number, and we can meet up later? I'll tutor you."

"Whatever. You better spend less time chasing the ladies and more time with your head in your book. I'm taking the highest grade."

"So testy," I mock.

"Why don't the two of you just fuck and get it over with," my best friend, Lincoln, says.

Glancing over my shoulder, I see that he, too, has moved seats so that he can hear my conversation with Charlotte.

"Not happening." Charlotte's practically seething. She turns around to face the front of the room, and I hold my fist out for Lincoln to knock.

"You really do get off on pissing her off, don't you?"

I shrug. "She makes it easy. It's not my fault she thinks she's better than everyone else. The last time I checked, we all put our pants on the same way."

Charlotte's shoulders stiffen, and I know I should feel bad for her hearing me, but I don't. When she slowly turns, there's a look in her eyes that I've never seen before.

"You know nothing about me, Spencer. Nothing. Some of us don't get to live off Mommy and Daddy's money without a care in the world." She turns back around, packs up her things, and slings her backpack over her shoulder. "Keep my name out of your mouth, and I'll do my best to stay away from you." She stalks out of class, even though there are five minutes left, and that's a very non-Charlotte thing for her to do.

"You did it this time, bro." Lincoln laughs.

The professor dismisses us, and I'm not going to lie. I look for her for the rest of the day. By the time I'm in bed later that night, I've pushed thoughts of Charlotte and her little speech into the back of my mind. She was just spouting off. That's what I tell myself as I let sleep claim me.

# Chapter ONE

I CAN'T BELIEVE THAT THIS day is finally here. In forty-eight hours, my little sister will be a married woman. While this is a happy occasion, I'm also so incredibly sad that our parents aren't here to see it happen. It's been ten years since we lost them, and although I manage their loss a little better each day, there's still a gaping hole in my heart. I miss them so much, and as we pull up to the beautiful Belisa Beach Resort in Florida, where my sister will start the next chapter of her life, that hole feels even more hollow than ever before.

"Wow, this place is incredible," Adeline, my sister's best friend, says as we exit the car.

"Right?" I agree with her.

The Belisa Beach Resort is oceanfront, and the views are absolutely stunning. I hope we'll manage to have a little bit of downtime so I can sit and enjoy the view. Maybe I'll get up early tomorrow, before the craziness of the day starts, and spend a few hours watching the sunrise on the beach or even the sunset after the rehearsal dinner. If I'm lucky, maybe I'll get to do both. Sure, I live near the ocean, but my job is so damn hectic, I don't have the time that I'd like to be able to just stop and enjoy it.

"What's first on the agenda?" Adeline asks.

"Today, nothing," my sister Audrey replies. "I thought we could maybe have dinner when everyone finally gets here, and then tomorrow we have our spa day, the rehearsal, and rehearsal dinner, and then Saturday, I say 'I do.'" She holds up her left hand and wiggles her sparkling diamond engagement ring. "I'm getting married!" she squeals and rushes me.

I hug her tight before releasing her, and she does the same with Adeline.

While we wait in line to check in, I send the best man and the bane of my existence, Spencer Pennington, a text message.

> **Me:** Did you bring the rings?
>
> **Spencer:** Wait? I thought you were bringing the rings.

I know he's just trying to rile me up. That's what Spencer does best. He's done it since the day we met freshman year at Clemson. How unlucky am I that my little sister met and fell in love with his best friend, Lincoln? Of all the men in the world, she had to fall in love with the best friend of my college rival.

> **Me:** Spencer.
>
> **Spencer:** I know you're rolling your eyes at me right now, Charlie.
>
> **Spencer:** That's hot.
>
> **Me:** Spencer!
>
> **Spencer:** Chill, woman. I have the rings.
>
> **Me:** Do you live your life to annoy me?
>
> **Spencer:** You need to loosen up, Charlie.

THE *Kissing* GAMES

I fight the urge to roll my eyes. Damn, insufferable man. I don't know how many times I've told him to call me Charlotte; he never listens. Only my friends call me Charlie. I don't bother to reply, instead slipping my phone back into my purse.

Audrey gets us checked in and passes us our room cards. "So, we're in a suite," she explains. "I was thinking the three of us could be in one room and Amara and Lorelei in the other. Until I get married, of course, and I join my man in the honeymoon suite, which is where Linc will be staying, while the guys have a suite similar to ours. Just a two-bedroom instead of a three."

The three of us head to our suite and start to get unpacked while we wait for the others to arrive. I'm thinking about a nap out on the beach when Audrey announces that everyone is here, well, everyone except for the groom. Apparently, Lincoln had a deal that he just had to close today and is driving down tomorrow.

Lincoln is a nice guy, but come on, who puts work before their wedding? This has been planned for months, and sure, I understand the concept of a big deal. My job is hectic right now as well, but I made it. I value my career. I busted my ass in college to get my degree, but there is nothing that would have stopped me from being here this weekend for my little sister.

Apparently, the groom doesn't feel that way.

It's just before nine when the five of us make our way to the restaurant at the resort, and I groan when I see Liam, Spencer, Tyler, and Jasper waiting at the entrance. "You didn't tell me they were joining us," I whisper-hiss to my sister.

She turns to glance at me over her shoulder. "They're a part of the wedding party. Of course they're joining us." She gives me a bright smile and turns back to greet the guys. I'm standing right behind her with Adeline, Lorelei, and Amara behind me. So, once Audrey steps back, I'm greeted by Liam.

He's such a sweet guy. "Hey, Charlie," he greets me. "It's good to see you."

"You too, Liam." I smile and return his quick hug. It's hard to believe that he and Lincoln share the same DNA. They are polar opposites in every way.

"Charlie," a deep masculine voice that sends tingles up my spine greets me. I don't have to look to know it's Spencer. I would recognize the deep timbre of his voice anywhere. I plaster a smile on my face and turn toward him.

"Spencer."

I'm taken off guard when he leans in and presses his lips to my cheek. "Good to see you."

I want to spout something like "Is it?" but I bite my tongue. I will not be the one to cause drama on the weekend of my baby sister's wedding.

I move down the line and say hi to Tyler and Jasper, who are also friends of the missing groom, before stepping out of the way and allowing the others to say hello. Once the pleasantries are out of the way, we're led to a large table in the back of the restaurant that will accommodate all of us.

I don't know how it happens, I should have been paying better attention, but I end up sitting with Audrey on one side of Spencer and me on the other. In my head, I'm cursing fate like a sailor. On the outside, I remain calm and act as if the seating arrangement doesn't annoy me. Hell, even Lorelei and Jasper aren't sitting next to each other and they're married. I can hardly complain.

"After all these years, I finally get to take you to dinner," Spencer says, leaning over into my space. His lips are next to my ear, and his hot breath fans across my cheek. I will not admit to anyone that heat spreads to my core from his nearness.

"What are you talking about?" I do my best to remain aloof.

"Dinner tonight. It's on the guys and me."

"When was this decided?" My tone is clipped when it should be anything but. It's actually a really sweet gesture, but I'll never tell him that.

"A few days ago. It was supposed to be our congratulations to the happy couple."

"But your best friend had more important things to do."

Spencer raises his hands and moves back into his space. "Don't take his shortcomings out on me," he says, reaching for his glass of water and taking a long pull.

I watch as his throat bobs as he swallows. When he returns his glass to the table, I quickly look away. Damn, Spencer Pennington. Why does the asshole have to be a sexy asshole? It really is a

THE *Kissing* GAMES

shame. He's hands-down one of the best-looking men I've ever laid eyes on. The messy dark hair, the tattoos that now reach his wrists. His voice is this deep timbre that makes you want to just drop your panties and ask what's next.

There is one major issue, though, one that's kept me from cashing in on any of his advances over the years. Spencer's kind of a dick. He's one of those guys who's been handed everything in life. Hell, in college, he barely had to crack open a book, and he was unprepared for class on most days, would laugh and stare off into space, and he still gave me a run for my money as the top of our class.

He doesn't know hardship or pain, and that makes him even more arrogant in my book. So, while the man might be a walking billboard for sex, it's one I'm going to continue to drive by.

Thankfully, I'm able to turn my attention to my sister and her friends and ignore the man sitting next to me. Well, mostly ignore. I feel his arm brush against mine when he reaches for the salt to put on his drink napkin that he could have just as easily asked me to pass him. I feel his arm on the back of my chair as we wait for our meals to be served and he's chatting with the guys. And I feel the heat of his hot breath when he leans in close to whisper how he's looking forward to spending the weekend with me.

So, maybe I don't ignore him, but I'm pretty certain he thinks that I am. That's why when he starts to draw circles on my bare shoulder, I stand abruptly and excuse myself to the restroom.

I take my time after doing my business to wash my hands and touch up my lip gloss. Hopefully, by the time I get back to the table, our food will be there, and we can eat and end this night. I'm fully aware that I'm going to have to be gracious and thank him, as well as the other guys, for dinner. The other guys, I don't mind so much, but Spencer's comment about finally buying me dinner hits a nerve.

Who am I kidding? Everything about Spencer Pennington hits a nerve with me. Knowing that I've stalled as long as I can, I take one last glance in the mirror before pulling open the bathroom door to head back to the table, only I'm not watching where I'm going, and I bump into someone.

"Easy, darlin'."

Shit. I know that voice.

With my hands plastered to his chest, I lift my gaze to find Spencer staring down at me. His arms are wrapped around my waist from where he kept me from falling, and the cocky expression I expect to find is nowhere in sight.

"Are you all right?" he asks softly, as his thumb gently caresses my hip.

"F-Fine. I'm fine," I say, pushing away from him. He keeps his hands on my hips until he's certain I'm steady before releasing me.

"You sure you're good?" he asks. His brow is furrowed as his gaze takes a lazy stroll over my body, checking for an injury.

"Yes. Sorry," I mumble. "I wasn't watching where I was going."

"I knew one day you would fall for me," he says, smirking.

And there he is. The cocky asshole I've known since our freshman year of college. Here I thought maybe there was a nice guy in there. I guess I was mistaken.

Don't get me wrong, Spencer isn't a terrible person, but there is just something about the two of us that's too much like oil and water. We just don't mix. In the ten years that I've known him, I don't remember us being able to just sit and have a normal conversation. Maybe the day we first met, but I was so preoccupied with all the drama in my life, I don't really remember. What I do remember is every instance after that, he was rude, and in turn, I snarked back. It's a game we play, and I have to say that we've mastered it.

"Are you ever going to grow up?" I ask him.

"Come on, Charlie, I'm all man. I can prove it to you. Tell me when and where. Should I get us our own suite?" He's grinning, and I hate that his grin is also sexy. Straight white teeth gleam at me, and the fact that I'm thinking about him being anything other than annoying just pisses me off further.

"I'm good." I step around him and head back to the table. Thankfully our meals are being delivered when I get there. I dive into my food and ignore Spencer as best as I can when he returns to his seat.

The remainder of the night is uneventful. Spencer doesn't bother me, and I do my best to ignore his presence beside me.

When the check is dropped off, the guys pull out their wallets and split it between the four of them.

"Thank you for dinner," Audrey tells them. "That was really sweet of you."

Spencer smiles at her. It's a genuine "aw, shucks. I'm one of the good guys'" smile. "You're welcome." He nods to Liam, Tyler, and Jasper. "We all wanted to do something for you all."

"We appreciate it."

"I can't fucking believe he's not here," Liam mumbles under his breath.

None of us let on that we heard him, but we all did. From the way the table grows quiet, my guess is that even his friends can't understand how he wouldn't already be here, but it is what it is, and there's no changing it now.

Much to my surprise, Spencer stands and pulls out my chair for me. I glance up at him, and he grins. "Thanks for having dinner with me, Charlie. Maybe next time it can just be the two of us?"

"You know she's never going to say yes, right?" Audrey laughs.

"Burn." The other guys in the group laugh good-naturedly.

"One day, Charlie Krause, one day you will say yes."

"Don't hold your breath. Oh, wait, do." I shrug as if I don't care either way. I don't want harm to come to the guy. I just want him to get over himself and stop using me as his target. I know he's not interested in me. He's been asking me out for years just to get under my skin, and I continue to turn him down. It's a game he likes to play, but he's too old for it. You know, like the parents who pretend that sitting in the kiddie pool in their backyard is for the sake of their kids when really, they're bringing back their childhood days.

Just like that.

Spencer Pennington will forever be the eighteen-year-old boy I met at freshman orientation in his mind. I don't ever see a day when that will change. And if that works for him, great. Perfect even. It doesn't, however, work for me. I'm twenty-eight years old. I don't have time for games. I want to build a life with someone. I can't believe I'm going to admit this, but I want what my little sister has found. Not a Lincoln. Their relationship leaves a little something to be desired. But that's just me.

No, I want a man who would move heaven and earth to be at every event of our wedding weekend. I want a man who is a hard worker, but also knows when the people you love need to come before your career. I get it, work can be hectic, and it's easy to lose yourself in that, but on the weekend you marry your forever love?

Nah, not for me. I won't settle until I find someone who wants to make me their world. I'm aware that my ideal unicorn may not exist, but I'm still hopeful that one day I'll find him, and we'll be able to have our very own happily ever after.

"Ladies, we'll walk you back to your room," Liam says.

"Oh, you don't have to do that," Audrey tells him.

"We insist," comes from Tyler.

We all chitchat on the way back to our suite. Once we reach the door, Audrey hugs each of them, and we all thank them again for dinner before disappearing inside.

"I'm beat. I'm going to go call Lincoln and go to bed," Audrey tells us. She's still smiling and upbeat, but it has to be bothering her that Lincoln isn't here like he's supposed to be.

We all agree that it's been a long day with travel, and we're all ready to get some sleep. However, once I'm in bed, I lie here for over an hour and can't seem to fall asleep. I don't know what's keeping me up, but I do know that the beach will be quiet this time of night, and I'm not passing up this opportunity.

Sneaking out of bed, I don't bother putting on a bra or even my flip-flops. I tiptoe out of our bedroom and make my way to the patio door that leads to the beach.

Downtime is not something I get much of, so I'm looking forward to just sitting in the sand, clearing my mind, and listening to the waves.

# Chapter TWO

Spencer

JASPER IS SNORING SO LOUDLY, I can't fall asleep. I've been tossing and turning for over an hour, and nothing is working. Slipping out of bed, I move to the couch in the living area of our suite, but as I walk by the patio door, another idea hits me.

The beach.

Living in Charleston, you'd think that I spent a lot of time on the beach, and trust me, I wish that were the case. My job is too demanding and life just has ways of keeping me from one of my favorite places. I love to listen to the sound of the waves crashing on the shore, and at this time of night, I'll have the beach to myself.

Decision made, I slide open the door as quietly as I can and slip into the night.

Standing at the edge of the shore, I let the waves wash over my bare feet as I dig my toes into the sand. Tilting my head back, I stare up at the night sky and exhale, feeling my body relax. I make a mental note to thank Lincoln and Audrey for choosing paradise to get married as I feel the stress of life fade into the sound of the ocean.

My job is stressful. Nothing I can't handle, but being CEO of a hospital takes its toll on you. It doesn't leave time for standing under the stars, digging your toes into the sand. I know part of that is my issue. My career is my life. I'm a single guy with no other responsibilities. It's easy to let my career swallow up all of my time. However, at this moment, work is the furthest thing from my mind.

Fuck, I love the ocean.

Not ready to head back inside, I decide to take a walk on the shore. I'm strolling along, enjoying the sound of the waves and nothing else, when I see a lone figure sitting on the sand. I continue my trek, planning to just wave and mind my own business. That plan gets tossed as soon as I see that dark auburn hair that, even in the moonlight, stands out like a sore thumb.

*Charlotte.*

Changing direction, I make my way to where she sits, just far enough away that the waves won't reach her. "Charlie."

She lifts her head, and the sneer that I expect isn't there. "Spencer."

"What brings you out here this time of night?" I ask.

"I could ask you the same thing."

"Jasper was snoring so loud, it sounded like a damn chainsaw. I couldn't sleep," I confess. My words cause a soft chuckle to escape her lips, and it's not the first time, and I'm damn sure it won't be the last that I recognize how beautiful she is. When she smiles, that beauty increases tenfold.

"I'm going to tell him that you said that." She gives me a pointed look.

I shrug. "I've got nothing to hide. He's lucky I didn't pour cold-ass water over his head." Taking a risk, knowing she's not a fan of mine, I plop down next to her in the sand. I leave some space between us, but I'm still sitting in what I'm sure she'll consider too close for comfort.

"Sure, have a seat. Join me," she replies sarcastically.

"Thanks." I lean my shoulder into hers, and I can see from the corner of my eye as she shakes her head. She doesn't yell at me, so that's a win. We sit in silence, neither one of us willing to end whatever this peace treaty is that's between us at the moment.

"I could sit out here all night," I finally say.

"Yeah," she agrees.

Glancing over, I see her eyes are closed, and her head is tilted back. The warm breeze has her hair whipping around her face. The urge to tuck those loose strands behind her ear is strong. The urge to lean over and capture her lips with mine is even stronger.

"Why are you staring at me?"

I smile. "What makes you think I'm staring at you?"

"I can feel you."

"Not yet, but you could." I let the innuendo fall freely.

"Ugh," she groans. She opens one eye and turns slightly to look at me. "Why are you here?"

"I told you. Jasper was snoring."

"Why are you *here*?" She points to the small area of sand between us. "Why are you sitting here with me, invading my quiet?"

"You're the one running that pretty mouth. I was content to just sit here and listen to the sound of the ocean and feel the night breeze."

She opens her eyes and dusts off her hands. "I'll leave you to it." When she starts to stand, I place my hand on her wrist.

"Stay."

"We're not friends, Spencer. Your best friend is marrying my little sister. This"—she points at herself and back to me—"is not what we do. This isn't us. It will never be us."

"Why?"

"What?" Her head rears back as if she can't understand how I could ask that question.

"Why are we not friends? Why is this"—I point at my chest and back at her just as she did—"not what we do?"

"We hate each other."

"Do we?" I don't hate her. I never have. She's always been out of reach, and she thinks she's better than everyone else—at least she did in college. I've not spent much time with her since. Hell, I didn't really spend time with her in college. She shot me down, and each time I asked after, I might have had a chip on my shoulder. I expected her refusal and made a game of it. What else was I supposed to do with the way she rejected me without reason or explanation? Okay, but I was a little full of myself back then, thinking I deserved either, but here we are, all these years later, and it still bothers me.

"Don't patronize me." This time when she stands, I don't stop her. "I love my little sister more than anything else in this entire world. I want her wedding to be everything she's ever dreamed of. You stay out of my way, and I'll stay out of yours." With those parting words, she storms off.

It takes everything in me not to chase after her. I want to demand she tell me what the fuck I did all those years ago for her to hate me. I don't bother, and I know the answer. Charlotte Krause is out of my league. She knows it. I know it. Everyone knows it. She has no qualms about flaunting it as well.

Instead, I keep my ass planted in the sand even though the appeal of this night vanished when Charlotte walked away from me. This is going to be a long-ass weekend.

When I finally made it back to our suite, my mind raced with thoughts of my interaction with Charlotte. I didn't even notice Jasper snoring, too caught up in my mind. It means I had a shit night's sleep.

When I hear Jasper move to the bathroom, I roll over and look at the clock. Just after eight. I got maybe three hours of sleep. It's going to be one long, exhausting day.

I realize we have the rehearsal this evening. I'll have to see Charlotte. That should piss me off, but it doesn't. Maybe I can make the best of this weekend. I can get her to tell me why she dislikes me so much. I'll either be successful or just piss her off even more. Either way, I'm going to do it.

"Hey," Jasper greets me. "Where did you disappear to last night?" He sits on the edge of his bed.

"Oh, you mean when you were snoring like a boar hog?" I ask. "How the hell has Lorelei put up with you for so long?"

"Fuck off," he grumbles. "Where did you go?"

"I went down to the beach."

"It's funny that we live by the beach and very rarely take the time to go there."

"That's why I was taking advantage of it," I tell him.

"What's on the agenda today?"

"Did you not get a copy of the email Charlie sent?" I ask him, rolling my eyes. "They have everything mapped out. I'm in charge of making sure the cake is good to go for tomorrow."

"She trusted you with the cake?" he asks, his eyebrows raised. It's not a secret that there is no love lost between Charlotte and me.

"Oh, I'm sure she's going to check on her own. She just needed to pretend to be spreading the duties since I'm the best man."

Jasper chuckles. "I can see that from her. What do we do until then?"

Before I can answer, my phone rings. When I see Lincoln's name, I grin. "You on your way?" I ask my best friend, who's also the groom.

"Not yet."

"What? Linc, man, you're getting married tomorrow. What in the hell do you mean not yet?" I ask him.

"This deal is taking longer to close than I anticipated."

"You're getting married." I shouldn't have to spell that shit out for him. Audrey is a cool girl, I like her for my buddy, but damn, she's going to be pissed he's not here yet.

"I'm working on it. Listen, can you tell Audrey for me? I tried to call her cell and couldn't get her. I'm headed into a meeting and won't be able to answer when she calls me back."

"Fuck that. I'm not telling your fiancée that you're going to be later than you thought. No way. Nope. Dude, you're sending me to do your dirty work."

"Spencer." His voice is pleading. "I don't have time to argue. Please just tell Audrey I'll call her as soon as this meeting is over. I'll be there. Just... tell her for me. Tell her I love her."

THE Kissing GAMES

"Fine. You owe me. You owe me big," I tell him.

"When you get married, I'll do the same for you."

"Fuck you. If and when I ever get married, there is nothing that's going to keep me from being involved."

"I've been working on this deal for months."

"You only get married once, brother," I remind him.

He sighs. "I have to go. Thank you. Tell Audrey that I love her, and I'll call her when I'm on my way."

"Fine." I end the call. I don't bother saying goodbye. This is going to suck.

"Is he really not on the road?" Jasper asks.

"Nope. Apparently, the deal is taking longer to close than he anticipated, and he's heading into a meeting. He claims that he tried to call Audrey to tell her, but she didn't answer and that he won't be able to answer while in his meeting when she calls him."

"Damn," Jasper mutters.

"This day is going to suck."

"Audrey's chill," he tells me.

"She is, but Linc can't expect her to keep chill about this. They're getting married." I shake my head in disgust. "I'm getting in the shower, and then I'm off to get my ass reamed by at least one Krause sister while the other is left to handle things on her own."

I'm standing outside of the girls' suite. I've raised my hand to knock three separate times, but each time I chicken out. I'm fucking exhausted and not in the mood to deal with getting my ass reamed because of my best friend. Knowing I can't stand out here like a creeper all day, I raise my hand and rap my knuckles against their door three times.

"I'll get it," a voice calls out. When the door opens, I find Charlotte standing there.

Her dark auburn hair is pulled up in a messy knot on the top of her head. She's wearing a tank top that shows off her tanned, toned belly, and the tiny scrap of material she's wearing that she's trying to pass off as shorts should be illegal. My eyes take their time roaming over every inch of her.

"If you're done eye-fucking me, do you mind telling me why you're standing at our door?" She crosses her arms over her chest, pushing her tits up, and my mouth waters.

Fuck, this woman is breathtaking.

"I need to talk to Audrey." As if saying her name summons her, she steps up beside her sister.

"Hey, Spence." She smiles at me.

I smile in return. "Hey, can we talk?"

"Sure, come on in."

I hesitate. I want to ask her to step into the hallway, but I don't know how she's going to react, and as much as I want to avoid sparring with Charlotte, I'm guessing her friends and sister need to be here to calm her down.

Stepping into their room, I smile and wave at the other ladies. "So, I, uh, talked to Linc this morning."

"Oh." Audrey's eyes light up.

*Fuck.*

"I tried to call him, but it went to voicemail. I figured he might be in a bad service area."

"Yeah." I reach up and grip my neck. "He's not on his way," I say, spilling the bad news as if I'm ripping off a Band-Aid.

"What?" Audrey asks. There's shock in her tone. Of course she's shocked. Her fiancé isn't here. They're getting married this weekend and he's MIA.

"He said it's taking longer than he thought to close the deal. I guess he tried to call you, but it went to voicemail." I hold my breath, not sure how she's going to react to the news.

"I forgot to charge it last night," Audrey confesses. "Did he say when he would be on his way?"

"No." I shake my head. "He said that he would call you when he was on his way."

She nods, turning to look at her sister and her friends. "It's fine. The rehearsal isn't until tonight, anyway. He'll be here in plenty of time."

"Audrey." Charlotte pulls her sister into a hug.

"I'm fine." Audrey offers a wide smile for her sister before turning back to me. "Thank you for relaying the message, Spencer."

"How are you so calm about this?" I ask her.

She shrugs, and as she turns to face me, she swallows hard before placing a smile on her face that doesn't reach her eyes. "He still has plenty of time to get here. We'll just carry on as we would, and then tonight we'll have the rehearsal, then dinner after, and tomorrow we live happily ever after."

"I expected tears and anger. Hell, even I got on him for not being on the road." How is she being so calm about this? If that was my fiancée, I'd be pissed as hell at her. This is their time. He's missing all of these moments with her. Hell, we're not even doing anything, but he's about to give her his last name and vow to love her for all eternity. He needs to be here for all of it. What's the point of all of this if he's not here? He could have just taken her to Vegas or to the fucking courthouse.

Audrey smiles softly, and it reminds me of her sister. "We both know how dedicated he is to his job. Is it bad timing? Sure, but it's not the end of the world. Everything will work out."

"What do you need from me today?" I ask her. I make a mental note to kick my best friend's ass for putting me in this position. He should be here. There is no excuse that's good enough. Not unless he's hurt or injured, and he's neither of those things.

"Charlie?" Audrey asks her sister.

"I have you down for verifying that the cake is all set with the resort bakery."

"Done. Anything else?"

"Not that I can think of," Charlotte replies.

"Do you ladies want to meet downstairs for brunch?"

"I'd love that. Thank you," Audrey pipes up before Charlotte has a chance to decline. "Give us thirty minutes, and we'll meet you in the lobby."

"We have our spa appointment, remember?" Charlotte gives her sister a pointed look. One that says, "what the hell are you doing?" and I fight my grin.

"That's not until eleven. We have plenty of time to grab something to eat first. It's nine thirty. We meet the guys at ten. That gives us an hour."

I can see that Charlotte wants to argue, but there's really nothing she can counter with. Audrey is right. There is plenty of time, and they have to eat.

"Bring it in," I tell her. I open my arms wide, and Audrey steps into them so I can give her a hug. "You're too good for him," I tell her. She laughs, and I release her. "You can bet your ass I'm going to continue to give him shit over this. He should have already been here."

I turn to Charlotte and open my arms for her. She rolls those beautiful blue eyes, just like I knew that she would. "One day, Charlie." I point my index finger at her and wink.

"Don't count on it," she mutters as I step out into the hallway, waving to the ladies as Charlotte shuts the door in my face.

That went better than I thought it would. I fire off a text to Lincoln as I reach our suite.

> **Me:**  I delivered your message. You don't deserve her. Get your ass here.

I don't wait for a reply because I know he's not going to risk looking at his phone during his meeting. I slide my phone into my pocket as I enter the suite to let the guys know we're having brunch with the ladies in less than thirty.

THE *Kissing* GAMES

# Chapter THREE

 *Charlotte*

BRUNCH WASN'T AS BAD AS I had anticipated it would be. The mood was somber even though my little sister smiled through it all, as if this was the happiest time of her life.

It's supposed to be.

The groom should have been there. I kept a smile on my face and let my little sister pretend everything was okay. My gut churned with a feeling that everything was not okay, but I hid it, thinking that maybe this time, my gut was wrong.

Outside of the groom not being here, today was fun. We spent the day at the spa, getting facials, massages, manicures, and pedicures, and ended with hair and makeup. We drank champagne and talked about anything and everything. We left our phones in a locker at reception, and to us, all was well. We all assumed that Lincoln had wrapped up his meeting and was on the road.

We were wrong.

He's not here. He hasn't even left South Carolina. I'm telling you, if my little sister didn't love the guy, I'd kick him in the balls, but I know Audrey wants to be a mom someday, so I'll have to keep my anger in check when I see him.

My little sister is smiling, but I can see the worry behind her eyes. To make matters worse, it's the rehearsal, and that means I have to lock arms with Spencer Pennington and smile as he leads me down the aisle.

Damn Audrey for falling in love with Spencer's best friend.

I just need to plaster a fake-ass smile on my face and get it over with—tonight and tomorrow—and then I'm done with him. I'm sure with my soon-to-be brother-in-law being his best friend, I'll see him again, unfortunately, but this week, is almost over. Less than forty-eight hours, and I'm free of Spencer.

"Best man and maid of honor," the wedding planner announces.

I step up to where she points, and I can feel Spencer next to me. I keep my eyes facing forward, waiting on further instruction. It's not like it's rocket science, but it gives me something to focus on outside of the sexy, infuriating man standing next to me.

"Link arms," the wedding planner instructs. Her tone tells me she's miffed that she even had to ask, but I ignore her and Spencer as long as I can.

"Yeah, Charlie. Let me guide you," Spencer says. I don't even have to look at him to know that he has a cocky smirk pulling at his lips.

Keeping my expression neutral, I slide my arm around his. I feel sparks ignite everywhere his body touches mine. I jolt at the intensity of his touch but hide it with a neutral expression. At least, I think I do.

When Spencer leans down and whispers, "I felt it too," I freeze. I don't realize that I'm holding my breath until the man himself calls me out on it. "Breathe, beautiful."

"I'm breathing," I say through gritted teeth. This time I turn and look at him. His dark brown eyes render me speechless. Why does he have to be, hands down, the best-looking guy I've ever seen?

"Your turn," the wedding planner tells us.

How, I don't know, but Spencer and I are in perfect sync as we start to slowly make our way down the makeshift aisle in the sand. "You want this one day?" he asks, making small talk.

"We're supposed to be smiling at the guests, not gossiping," I snip.

His deep chuckle washes over me, and I feel it from my head to my toes. "I think your kitty needs petting, Charlie. You're too uptight."

"I'm not uptight. This is my baby sister's big day, and I want it to be perfect. And I'm allergic to cats," I snap. Yes, I'm well aware he's not talking about *that* kind of kitty, but I can't go there. Not today, and not with him.

"Somebody should tell the groom that," he mutters under his breath.

I stop when we reach the arch of flowers and turn to face him. I want to tell him that I agree with him, but that goes against every fiber of my being, so instead, I just give him a curt nod and take my place where I'll stand up with my sister.

I keep my eyes trained on Audrey as she makes her way toward the altar. My heart squeezes in my chest, and I wish my parents were here to see this. To see the amazing woman that my little sister turned out to be. The ache I feel for all that they've lost, for all that Audrey and I have lost, is deep.

They say that time heals all wounds, and while I can somewhat agree with that, I also disagree. I miss them every single day. There isn't a day that goes by that I don't want to call one or both of them for advice or give them good, and hell, even bad news. I miss their presence in our lives, and yes, while the days go by, it's a little easier to breathe, but that ache, that tenderness deep in my soul, always remains.

Keeping my eyes on the aisle, I wait for Audrey to come walking down by herself. Anger flares in my gut when I once again think about everything that Lincoln is missing out on. This is a day they're supposed to experience together. A moment in time when they prepare to spend the rest of their lives with each other, and he's not here. I hate that for my sister. It worries me to think about what else Lincoln will miss out on in their marriage. Anniversaries, birthdays, the birth of their children? I want better for her, but this is her choice. I can't make this decision for her. Not that I would want to. However, if I were the one to choose her forever, it wouldn't have been Lincoln. It would have been someone more like... Liam.

As if the universe can hear my thoughts, Audrey walks down the aisle. My eyes turn to Liam, and he's got a soft smile pulling at the corner of his mouth, and his eyes are glued to her. He's watching her while her gaze is trained on the arch of flowers. When she reaches her place, and Lincoln's void is obvious, Liam steps forward. He leans over and whispers something in my sister's ear, making her smile, and that one, it's real. There's no worry behind her eyes, and yeah, I think, not for the first time, that my sister chose the wrong brother.

We do a quick run-through of how tomorrow is supposed to go. Liam assures everyone that he will make sure Lincoln knows his part. I have to fight like hell not to roll my eyes.

Liam jokingly asks Audrey if she wants to run away with him, and while one of the other ladies belts out her approval, I'm silently sending her mine, hoping that the universe will take control and make that happen.

Spencer grumbles about being hungry and some other random comment about winning me over tonight. He can shit in one hand and wish in the other and see which one fills up faster. There will never be a world in which Spencer Pennington "wins me over."

A few hours later, Adeline and I are sitting at the bar. She's flirting with this hot bartender, Decker, and I'm content to just be here for the show.

"He's hot." I nod my approval once Decker refills our drinks then walks away.

Adeline watches as he begins to clean up at the other end of the bar. "Yep."

I toss my head back in laughter. "You going to make your move?"

"What? No. I'm just here for the booze, and the eye candy is just a bonus."

"I think you should ask him to meet up later, or hell, tomorrow after the wedding."

"Ladies." I hear from beside me, and I don't even bother to hide my groan at that voice.

"Spencer, I believe your table is over there." I point to the corner of the room where the guys have been sitting at a table, tossing back drinks.

"Let me buy you a drink," he whispers huskily.

"I'm good."

"You planning on letting the bartender pet your kitty?" he asks.

I would never admit this out loud, but his question has heat pooling between my thighs. "Told you, I'm allergic. Besides, he's spoken for." I nod toward Adeline, and I realize in my buzzed state that I just threw her under the bus.

"Hey, man, what can I get you?" The bartender, Decker, stops to stand in front of Spencer.

"A refill for the ladies and another round for the table," he tells him.

"Coming right up." Decker's eyes flow over to Adeline, and he winks at her before he gets busy filling Spencer's order.

"Maybe you should focus on making sure your best friend gets here and less on buying me a drink."

"He's on his way." A dark look passes over his face.

"That." I point at him. I'm a little buzzed, but not so much that I didn't notice the change in him. "What's that about?"

"Nothing."

"You can't bullshit me, Spencer. What is that look?"

He sighs and leans his elbows on the bar. His dark brown eyes study me, and I can see what appears to be a storm brewing. "He should fucking be here. He should have been the first one of us to arrive. I hate that Audrey is doing this shit on her own." His tone of voice, although low, is just for the two of us. I can hear that he truly is pissed at his best friend.

I'm not sure what to do with that. I don't know this side of Spencer. He's never let me see this part of him before in all the years I've known him.

"I can't believe I'm about to say this, but I agree with you," I mutter before downing the rest of my drink.

He leans in close, his lips a breath from mine. "Just the beginning, beautiful Charlie."

"What?" I pull my head back. He's close. Too close.

"I'm wearing you down. First, it's you agreeing with me, telling me I'm right. Next, it will be dinner and drinks, and then, maybe if I'm lucky, I'll get to pet your kitty," he says. His deep voice is low and husky, and damn him, my panties are ruined.

"You have a cat?" Liam asks, walking up to join the conversation. "I thought you were allergic?"

Spencer stands to his full height and, if I'm not mistaken, takes a step closer to me. "How in the hell do you know she's allergic to cats?" he asks. His tone is different, commanding. "And what are you doing? I told you I was buying us another round."

"You took too long," Liam replies easily. "And Audrey told me she was allergic."

"Here you go." Decker is back with our drinks. He serves Adeline and me first, then slides four bottles toward Spencer as he hands over his card to pay.

"Thank you for the drink, Spence," Adeline says with a kind smile.

"You're welcome," he tells her, but his eyes are on me.

Ugh. I hate the thought of having to thank him for anything, but I do so begrudgingly. "Thank you for the drink, Spencer." I refuse to shorten his name. That admits that there's a level of familiarity between us that's not there. We're acquaintances at best. College rivals, who've been thrown into this situation by my sister and his best friend. That's all that we will ever be.

"Your pleasure is mine, Charlie." He winks, grabs his bottle of beer, and follows Liam back to their table.

"Damn," Adeline mutters.

"What?" I turn to look at her, thankful that it's dark in the bar and she can't see the flush on my pale cheeks, and if she does, hopefully, she chalks it up to the alcohol I've consumed.

"I could feel the sparks from here."

"Sparks?" I raise my eyebrows like I have no idea what she's talking about. It's lies. All lies because I felt those sparks too. I still

THE *Kissing* GAMES

feel them deep in my core, but I refuse to acknowledge them. I'm shutting this shitshow down.

"He's into you."

"He's into women."

"Last I heard, you were a woman," she teases.

"You know what I mean. There is nothing special about me to Spencer Pennington. I'm a challenge for him. Everything always comes easy to him. I turned him down the first day of freshman year, and he's been a pain in my ass ever since."

"Really? That long?"

"Yep."

"Have you ever asked yourself why?"

"What do you mean?" Even in my inebriated state, I think she's had too much to drink. I should convince her that this is our last one.

"Why, after all these years, is he still trying? Why is he still a pain in your ass? Or is he?" she says, her voice all sly. I don't know what that means exactly, but it sounds good in my head.

"He's still trying because he lives to annoy me. Yes, he's still, to this very day, a pain in my ass."

"I think it's a unique brand of foreplay."

"What?" I whip my head to face her and almost fall off my stool. I have to hold onto her arm, which makes her crack up laughing for some reason. I'm barely settled back in my seat when I feel a hand on my back. Not just any hand, but his hand. Don't ask me how I know. It just is what it is.

"You okay, Charlie?"

"Oh, she's fine as frog hair." Adeline laughs. "Actually, Spence, I think you need to take her up to the suite. She's had one too many, if you know what I mean."

"What?" It seems to be the only word I can form at the present moment.

"Come on, Charlie." Spencer's voice is soft as he offers me his hand.

"I'm not leaving." I glare at him, then turn my glare on Adeline. "You can't stay down here by yourself."

"I'm a big girl," she counters.

"I'll make sure she gets to her room." Liam appears beside us.

"Liam can walk us."

"I'm not ready to leave yet," Adeline says, and I can see the determination in her eyes. She's not coming with me, and the man standing next to me with his big hand on my back is stubborn enough not to leave until I do. He wants to torture me with his presence all the way back to our suite.

I glare at her, but she just grins, sipping her drink. Speaking of drinks, I grab mine from the bar and tilt it back, draining the glass. If I have to spend any amount of time with Spencer on my own, I'm going to need it.

Placing the empty glass back on the bar, I slide off the stool, only to wobble. I reach out to steady myself, and it's Spencer's arm that I find for my balance. Damn, I didn't think I drank that much. I know the guys had more than us, they all came up several times for rounds of beers and shots, and Decker delivered some as well. How is he standing straight? I almost ask him but decide I don't really care. Just something else that Spencer Pennington seems to come out on top with.

I wonder if he shits gold and glitter, too, since his life seems to be full of it?

A deep chuckle pulls me out of my thoughts. "No gold or glitter, baby. I'm human, just like you." He smiles down at me.

"I'm not your baby," I slur.

"I'm taking her to the suite. I'll see you guys later," Spencer says. Then he turns to look at Liam. "You got Adeline?"

"Yeah, I'll make sure she gets back safe."

"How are you walking straight?" I ask Spencer as he guides me out of the bar.

He just chuckles as he pulls me a little closer, and we head to my suite that I'm sharing with the girls. We're quiet on the walk, and I'm suddenly exhausted.

"You smell good," I mumble.

"So do you," he replies softly.

THE *Kissing* GAMES

When we reach our door, I struggle to get my key out but finally manage to hold it up in the air. Spencer smiles down at me. Something not a lot of men do. I'm tall at five foot eight, but I feel tiny next to him.

"You going to be okay?" he asks. He tucks a stray piece of hair behind my ear.

"I'll be fine." I wave him off. I turn and attempt to insert the keycard into the door and have no luck.

"Let me."

I don't have time to move out of the way before he's pressing his body next to mine. Reaching around me, he takes the keycard and unlocks the door.

"Call me if you need me."

"I won't need you."

"Yeah, but if you do, promise you'll call."

"You're going to be mad that you were nice to me when you wake up, and the haze of the alcohol is gone." I point a finger at him. At least, I think I do. I might have pointed two. It's all a little fuzzy.

"I'll never regret you, Charlie," he says softly. With his hand over mine, he pushes the door the rest of the way open and motions for me to head inside. I do, and to my surprise, he follows me.

"What are you doing?"

"You need to hydrate, and you need to take something for that hangover you're bound to have in the morning."

"I'm fine. And if I need to, so do you."

He just grins, walks past me to the small kitchen, fills me a glass of water, and grabs the bottle of headache medicine that's sitting on the counter, which I'm sure my sister or Lorelei left for their hangover maintenance before they went to bed.

"You need help getting to bed?" he asks.

"No."

He nods. "Call me if you need me."

"I won't."

He nods and takes a couple of long strides until he's standing next to me. He bends and shocks the hell out of me, leaving me speechless when he presses his lips to my forehead. "Sweet dreams, Charlie."

He turns and walks out of the room before I can even wrap my head around what just happened, and damn it, he's still calling me Charlie.

# Chapter FOUR

Spencer

MY CHEST ACHES AS MY heart hammers like a bass drum. With each step that we take toward the suite the ladies are staying in, the beat intensifies, as does the ache. Lifting my hand, I rub over my heart to try to ease the pain.

It doesn't work.

I could strangle Lincoln. It's a good thing he's not here because I'd kick his ass. Not because he called off the wedding—you have to follow your heart—but Lincoln knew before this morning. His pussy ass was stalling, and now, here we are, standing outside the suite of his now ex-fiancée and her friends and sister to give them the news.

I still might kick his ass when I get home. He should have been man enough to admit this wasn't what he wanted. Things should never have gotten this far. Lincoln is on my shit list. What's worse is that Charlotte already hates me. It's been years, and I don't know where the hate came from, but it's there, and this—me being involved in breaking her sister's heart—is just going to make that hate fester and grow.

I'm definitely kicking his ass when we get home.

"I really don't want to fucking do this," Liam says, his head hanging.

Reaching out, I place my hand on his shoulder. None of us wants to do this. That's why we're all here. We decided to come as a united front. We don't agree with how Lincoln handled this situation, and we want the ladies behind that door to know that. We also want them to know that whatever they need, we're here for it.

"We're with you," Ty tells Liam.

He nods, lifts his head and then his hand, and raps his knuckles against the door. I can hear laughter and excited voices behind the door, and my gut twists knowing that we're about to take that away.

When the door opens, Liam steps into the room. Audrey is immediately on her feet, her eyes locked on Liam, asking what's wrong as we all file into the room behind him. Liam uses the softest tone I've ever heard from him when he tells Audrey that she should sit down.

Stubborn like her sister, she refuses. "Just say it," she says, and I can already hear in her voice she knows what's coming.

I think deep down, we all knew that this was coming. Why else would he put his job over his wedding? A wedding that's been in the works for months? We didn't want to believe it. I know I didn't. I was pissed at him putting her second to his career. I told him as much. However, in a million lifetimes, I never imagined he would do this. At least not hours before they were supposed to promise to love each other for a lifetime.

Yeah, definitely going to be kicking his ass when we get home.

The guys and I surround Liam as he breaks the news to Audrey that Lincoln's not here, and he's not going to be. He's a coward. She argues that he was on his way, and I bet a year's salary he was never on his way. He didn't drive halfway and turn around.

He lied.

Audrey loses her battle with her tears, and the look on Liam's face can only be described as devastation. That's when I realize

that he's in love with her. The way he's looking at her, the heartache at seeing her tears, he's crushed that the woman he loves is in pain from his jackass brother. We all know that Liam met Audrey first since he was saving Lincoln's ass back in the day on their first date. Liam had to cover for him because his ass was running late. He should have whisked her away from that restaurant. The look on his face tells me he's thinking the same thing. Fury and pain, all wrapped into one. That's what the younger West brother is feeling at this moment.

Charlotte pulls Audrey from Liam's arms and hugs her tight. She whispers to her sister as she closes her eyes, and a lone tear trails over her cheek. I tighten my fists at my sides to keep from reaching out and capturing it with my thumb. Lincoln is breaking more than one heart today.

I've known Charlotte Krause since our freshman year of college. I've seen her pissed, happy, smiling, studious, focused, and determined. I've never seen her sad. The sight of that lone tear has all of my protective instincts I didn't know I had, standing tall.

They stand tall for her.

Audrey pulls away from her sister and begs for Liam to go. I can see the anguish on his face. The last thing he wants to do is leave her when she's upset. She tells him again that she needs him to leave. She's frantic, and it's like a knife in the chest to watch her pain.

I put my hand on Liam's shoulder. "We can do that," I tell her. I know without prompting, Liam won't leave her, but that's what needs to happen. We need to let her sister and her friends support her through this while we take care of everything else. I tell him that, and he gives a slow nod.

It's Charlotte who speaks.

"Thank you," she says softly, and she places her hand on my arm, giving it a gentle squeeze. It's the softest she's ever spoken to me in all the years I've known her. The heat of her small hand against my arm is searing. It's the first time she's ever touched me on her own accord.

I want to hold her. I want to pull her into my chest, wrap my arms around her, and tell her that it's all going to be okay. I know she's not the one that was getting married, but I feel as though I need to be the one she leans on while she holds the weight of her sister's pain on her shoulders.

With a nod, the guys and I guide Liam out of the suite. His shoulders are tight, and he's walking with purpose. Part of me wishes Lincoln were here to be on the receiving end of his brother's wrath, and then the other part knows that wouldn't be a good idea because Charlotte's lone tear pops into my mind, and my vision blurs. He wouldn't be faring well if he were here.

Knowing that Liam's barely holding on, I guide him outside and around the building. He lets out a roar and smashes his fist against the building. "Motherfucker!" he roars.

Ty, Jasper, and I stand back and watch as he bows his head, his chest heaving with anger. We don't interfere, letting him do his thing. When he finally lifts his head, his eyes are wet with emotion.

"How?" His voice is raspy, and he doesn't try to hide the broken pieces. "What kind of man stands the woman he's supposed to love up on their wedding day? How could he do this to her? To Audrey? If he didn't love her, he should have told her. He should never have let it get this far. Fuck!" he screams and runs his fingers through his hair.

"We all agree with you, man," Ty says, his voice low and even.

"He's a coward," Jasper says.

I know I should speak up, but I can't. All I can see is the devastation on Audrey and Charlotte's faces. I'm sure the other ladies were just as upset, but those two were my focus. My mind keeps replaying that single tear rolling down Charlotte's cheek, and I fight the urge to run back to her to make sure she's okay. Not that she would let me.

"We need to tell your parents and their aunt Miranda," I tell Liam.

"I'll tell my parents." Liam sighs.

"I'll go with you," Jasper tells him.

"We'll go talk to Miranda," Ty speaks up.

I want to tell him that Jasper can go with him. That's all I need, for another member of Charlotte's family to hate me right now. Knowing I don't have a choice, I nod my agreement. I told her that we would take care of everything outside of the suite, and I meant it.

"I have the wedding planner's number," I say, already reaching for my phone in my pocket. As best man, Charlotte and I had to talk with her more than I liked, but now, I'm glad that I have a way to reach her without having to search the entire resort to find her.

Liam nods. "I'll talk to Mom and Dad and then call you to see where you are. I don't know if the wedding planner will need help, but there are guests that are here from out of town, and someone has to break the news to them. I don't know how to get the word out, and maybe the wedding planner has a contact list and room numbers."

"If we have to go door to door, that's what we'll do." I made Charlotte a promise, and I intend to keep it. She's going to text me and want an update, and I want to be able to assure her that I've got it under control. All she needs to worry about is being there for her sister. We can clean up our friend's mess, but it's the last fucking time. In fact, if he ever does get married, he can count me out. Fuck this. He knew. I know that he knew, and he waited until the last possible moment to tell us, so we could be the courier of his bad news. Lincoln and I have been best friends since college, but fuck me. I really don't like him right now.

"Let's get this over with," Liam mutters. He digs his phone out of his pocket and taps at the screen before placing it to his ear. "Hey, Dad. Where are you?" He listens, and his eyes find mine. "Okay, the guys and I are coming to join you." Another pause to listen. "See you soon." He ends the call and slides the phone back into his pocket. "They're having breakfast. Miranda is with them."

I exhale a heavy breath. "Lead the way." This time as we make our way to drop the news a second time, my chest is still tight, my heart is still beating its own form of a rock song in my chest, but my anger is intensified.

When we reach the restaurant, Liam's parents and Miranda are all smiles until they see the look on our faces.

"What's happened?" his mom asks.

Liam opens his mouth and quickly clamps his jaw shut, shaking his head. I clear my throat and drop the bomb on them. "Linc's not coming."

"What?" their dad asks. "What do you mean he's not coming?"

"He called yesterday and said he was finally on the road, but this morning he called, and he's not coming."

"Was there an accident? Is he hurt? Sick?" his mom asks.

"He's sick alright," Liam seethes. "He knew," he spits, barely containing his anger. "He knew he was going to do this and lied to us. Lied to her. He told her he was on his way, on the road, and headed here, but he was still in Charleston. He never planned to be here, and he waited until today to tell us."

His mom covers her mouth, and her eyes are wide. His dad looks like he's going to be in line behind Liam and me to kick Lincoln's ass, and Miranda is just sitting there staring. "Charlie is with Audrey. The other ladies too," I say. She nods. "They're taking good care of her," I reassure her. She simply nods again.

"Lincoln." I hear a deep grumbling voice. I turn my head to see their dad with his phone to his ear. "What's going on, son?" he asks. I watch as Mr. West's face falls. He listens to what my best friend is saying on the other line. Time seems to stand still as he sits and listens. "I'll see you at home." Mr. West's voice is hard as he ends the call and places his phone face down on the table.

"Well?" Liam asks him.

Mr. West shakes his head. "What do we need to do?" he asks instead of answering Liam's question.

"I'm going to call the wedding planner and let her guide us."

"We'll help with anything that we can." He looks at Miranda. "I am so sorry about all of this."

She shrugs. "It's not your fault. Things happen." She takes a sip of her orange juice and pushes back from the table. "I'm going to go say hi to my nieces. I'll be ready to leave when you are," she tells them.

My jaw goes slack as I watch her lack of emotion. Is this what Audrey and Charlotte grew up with? I know they lost their parents years ago, from what Lincoln told me when all this wedding stuff started, and he told me I'd have to be working with Charlotte as she was the maid of honor. I didn't ask questions, and now I wish that I had. Part of me wanted to hear it from Charlotte. I wanted her to tell me, even though I knew my chances of that happening were slim to none.

Ten years I've known her, and that beautiful, sassy woman has kept me on my toes the entire time. Shaking out of my thoughts, I send off a text to the wedding planner, and immediately my phone starts to ring.

"Spencer," I answer.

"Are you pranking me?" she asks.

"I wish I were. He's not here, and he's not coming. The wedding is off. Tell me what I need to do." I need this done and over so I can report back to Charlotte and, if I'm lucky, give her that hug that I've been craving since the moment I saw that tear roll down her cheek.

"Okay. I've got this," the wedding planner replies.

"Do you have a list of guests' room numbers?" She works for the resort, so I'm hoping she has a list or at least has access to a list.

"I do. I'm going to type up something so that we can slide it beneath their doors. It's going to save time and keeps us from having to explain to everyone. I'll just tell them the wedding will not be moving forward, and the family of both the bride and the groom send their deepest apologies and appreciate all of their love and support."

"It was him," I tell her.

"What?"

"Lincoln. He called it off. Audrey has nothing to apologize for."

"Right, well, it's my job not to choose sides, Mr. Pennington. I'm typing it up as we speak," she says, and I can already hear her fingers flying across the keys of her laptop. "There." She proceeds to read her statement, and although I hate that it sounds as if Audrey is apologizing, I agree that it's sufficient for its purpose.

"That works. Now what?"

"These are printing, and I'll get to work notifying the guests. If you have anyone who has not checked in yet, I'll be sure that they are notified as well. If I remember correctly, everyone in attendance was staying at the resort, and there were no locals."

"That's correct." I'm thankful for Charlotte and the fact that I listened when she talked during the planning of all of this to know the answer to that question.

"I'll take care of the rest. That's my job. You just take care of her, yeah?" she says, her voice softer.

"We've got her," I assure her. "Call or text if I can help in any way."

"It's under control."

"She's taking care of it." I go on to tell them about the statement, and Mrs. West looks relieved.

"Now what?" Liam asks.

"We check on the girls? We support Audrey in any way that we can. Get her drunk? Drive back to Charleston and kick his ass? Fuck, man, I don't know what we do." I glance at Mrs. West. "Sorry." I wince when I realize I dropped the F-bomb.

She waves me off. "Been married to this one for far too many years and raised two rowdy boys. I'm used to it." She gives me a kind smile. "Boys, sit down and eat something," she encourages us.

"Not all that hungry, Mom," Liam replies.

"Sit." His dad commands. "Eat, and then you all can go check on her."

So, we sit. We order food and eat silently as we all process today's turn of events, which isn't at all what we had planned. Thirty minutes later, we're headed back to the girls' suite. Audrey isn't there.

"She's in her room," Charlotte says sadly. "She just needed some time to be alone and to process everything."

Liam nods. The hurt he feels is palpable.

"You doing okay?" My voice is soft, my question just for her.

"I'm doing okay. I hate this for her. I hate that she's hurting, and I can't fix it. I hate that she was close to having a family, and now she's stuck with me, just me."

"Hey." I can't fucking take it. I slide my arm around her waist and pull her into my chest. I expect a fight but get none as she shudders a deep breath. I hold her until she pulls away and takes a step back. "We'll get through it like we always do," she assures me.

We stay and chat awkwardly for a few more minutes, not really sure what to say. Jasper has his arms around his wife, Lorelei. Ty is sitting on the edge of the couch with his hand on Amara's shoulder. I'm standing as close to Charlotte as she'll let me, and Liam, he's on the chair, hands covering his face as he works through his hurt and anger with his brother.

My best friend really knows how to fuck things up.

THE *Kissing* GAMES

# Chapter FIVE

 *Charlotte*

Today has been a clusterfuck of epic proportions. Audrey insisted she needed some time for herself and sequestered herself in the bridal suite she was supposed to be sharing with her husband.

I feel... antsy. There is nothing I can do to make this better for her, and it's killing me. My mind won't stop racing with all the questions. Why did he let things get this far? How is she really doing? Will this turn her away from love? And the biggest, are our parents watching over us? Are they seeing this? Will they be able to silently help her navigate this, because she keeps assuring me that she's fine and just needs time, but how can she be fine? Her fiancé left her on the day of their wedding.

Lincoln West is an asshole.

"That we can agree on," a deep voice says from beside me.

I don't need to turn to see who it is, and I know *his* voice. However, I do turn to glance at him. "I guess I said that out loud, huh?" I ask, taking another sip of my drink. It's something fruity and delicious, and even though I can't taste the alcohol, I know it's there. I need to slow down. I'm not a big drinker, but after the day I've had... that we've all had, I felt a few drinks were in order.

"You did," Spencer says, leaning his shoulder into mine. "And like I said, that we can agree on."

"Have we ever done that?" I tilt my head to the side. "Have we ever agreed on anything?"

He grins, and his brown eyes sparkle, and his broad smile seems to brighten up the dimly lit bar. "I think this is our first time, Charlie." He winks, and that one simple action sends a swarm of butterflies that takes flight in my belly.

I place my hand over my stomach to try and stop the feeling. I don't want my body to react to him. Not him. Not Spencer. "You think you're cute." I point at him with the index finger of the hand that's holding my glass.

He leans in close, and I pull in a deep breath as his scent—something woodsy—surrounds me. "No, but I know you are," he replies huskily.

*No. No. No.* I pretend to ignore him, and I definitely ignore my body's reaction to him being this close to me. I uncross and cross my legs, hoping to alleviate some of the tension between my thighs. "Why are you here?"

"Beautiful Charlie. How much have you had to drink? You know why we're here." He's smiling at me, and I have to bite down on my cheek to keep from returning the gesture.

Once I'm composed, I glance over at him so he can see me roll my eyes. "Why are you sitting here at the bar next to me? Why are you not with the guys?"

"Honestly, you were sitting here all alone, and I didn't like it." He shrugs as if his reply doesn't render me speechless.

"Charlotte!" a voice calls out. I turn to see Amara waving her hands at me. "We miss you," she calls across the bar.

I can't help but smile and shake my head. We've all decided to indulge ourselves a little tonight, and my sister's friends are well on the path of nursing hangovers tomorrow. I wave and stand, sliding off the stool and grabbing my half-empty glass. I don't say a word to Spencer as I walk away from him. This time it's not because I don't want to, but it's because I don't know what to say. He's tilted the scales of our... relationship, if that's what you want to call it, and I don't know how to handle that. I know what to do with his barbs and his flirty one-liners, but tonight, they're not just flirty. He's mixed in a little sweet, and that is not something I was prepared for.

I reach the table and take the empty seat next to Amara. She leans over, giving me a one-armed hug, and then stands again, calling out for the guys to join us. *Great. Just what I need. More time with Spencer.* At least everyone else will be here to be our buffer.

"You feeling good, darlin'?" Ty asks, smiling at Amara.

She steps away from the table and closes the short distance between them. I watch as he stares down at her, his eyes boring into hers. She places her hands on his chest and then turns her head. She scans the bar and lands on a table of guys sitting not far from us. "Not yet, but I plan to be." She nods toward the table and walks away from him.

I stifle a laugh when I watch as she puts a little extra sway in her hips. We all know it's for Tyler's benefit, and by the way his eyes follow her every move, I'd say he's enjoying the show.

Spencer drops into the chair next to mine.

"Why are you following me?" I ask him.

"Just hanging out with friends," he replies, sipping from his bottle of beer.

"Well, go over there." I point to the other end of the table where Lorelei and Jasper are sitting. She looks miserable, and Jasper, well, he just looks as if the world is sitting on his shoulders.

I study them, and when Jasper holds his hand out to his wife, I hold my breath, waiting to see what Lorelei will do. Her eyes are full of what looks like pain and the love she has for him. Just when I think she's going to deny him, she places her hand in his and allows him to help her to her feet. My eyes follow them as Jasper pulls her into his hold and wraps his arms around her.

They don't portray the happy couple at this moment, but they're here together, and the way she grips the back of his shirt, and the possessive way he places his palm on the small of her back, it has me longing for that. For more.

Lorelei rests her head on his shoulder. Her eyes are closed, but that doesn't stop the lone tear from sliding down her cheek. I feel her pain. We're not close, but the emotions of the private moment between husband and wife are palpable.

Quickly, I look away, feeling guilty for intruding on their moment. "He's been off all weekend," Spencer says, nodding in their direction. "We're rooming together."

"They love each other," I say, glancing back at the couple who are still tightly embracing on the dance floor.

"You ever been in love, Charlie?" Spencer asks.

His question floors me. This isn't us. We don't do this. "Nope," I say, popping the *p*. I don't want to talk about this with him. "You?" I find myself asking. Suddenly, for the first time in ten years, I'm hanging on to his every word.

"I thought I could have been once," he confesses.

I can't help it. I have to turn to look at him. There's a shy smile, something I've never seen from this man, pulling at his lips. "I can't believe I'm going to even ask this, but what happened?" I have this deep-rooted need to know his answer.

He shrugs. "I was interested. She wasn't."

It must be the alcohol in my system because I find myself reaching over and placing my hand on his arm. "It's her loss," I tell him.

His eyes widen with surprise, but he quickly masks it with a stiff nod. The moment is awkward but not uncomfortable, oddly enough. I lift my glass to my lips and take a small sip. Averting my gaze, I look at the other side of the table at Adeline. Her fingers are flying across the screen of her phone.

"Your dad?" I ask her.

She nods. "Who else," she grumbles as the sexy bartender walks up and places his hands on the back of her chair. She tilts her head back and smiles shyly at him, placing her phone face down on the table.

THE *Kissing* GAMES

"How's it going?" Decker, the sexy bartender, asks. He's wearing a playful smile that causes Adeline's cheeks to flush a soft pink. Then again, that could just be the lighting.

"Good," I answer him, and Adeline nods.

"Can I get you all anything?" he asks.

I watch as his thumb slides gently over Adeline's bare shoulder. I expect her to freeze, but her shoulders fall as if his touch relaxes her.

Huh, I'm definitely going to have to ask my roommate what that's all about.

Lifting my glass, I drain it and push back from the table to stand. "I need a refill, but I'll follow you to the bar. Adeline?" I ask her. It's just the three of us currently sitting at the table.

"I'm good. Thank you."

That leaves Spencer. We're in some kind of weird being nice thing tonight, so I turn to him. "Spencer?"

"I'll come with you," he says, standing to his full height.

I tilt my head back to look up at him. "I can bring it back."

"This round's on me, Charlie."

"No."

He leans in, placing his lips next to my ear. "Yes."

I shiver, and the way his brown eyes smolder tells me that he didn't miss my body's reaction to him. "Fine," I huff. "Whatever. You can buy your own drink, and I'll buy mine."

"She always like this?" I hear Decker ask him.

I whip my head around, and Decker winks at me. That's when I feel Spencer's hand on the small of my back as he tugs me into his side. "She keeps me on my toes," is his reply.

What in the hell is he talking about, and why is he touching me like... like I'm his? I don't have too much time to ponder this before we reach the bar. Spencer pulls a stool out for me and nods for me to sit. I don't do it because he tells me to. I do it because these heels are killing my feet.

"Hey." A female bartender stops in front of us. "What can I get you?" she asks Spencer.

I roll my eyes because, of course, she would ask him first. He's never not had all the ladies batting their eyelashes for him, ready and willing for whatever piece of himself he's willing to give them for however long he's willing to give it.

"Charlie?" Spencer says, and I look over at him. "What do you want, darlin'?"

I open my mouth and then quickly close it, only to open it again and repeat the same process. He's asking me? Putting me first? Spencer Pennington?

"Charlie?" He bends so he can look me directly in the eye. "You good?"

"Yes." I nod and sit up a little straighter on the stool. "Strawberry daiquiri." My voice is so low I'm not even sure he heard me.

He stands to his full height. "Strawberry daiquiri for my girl and a Busch Light for me," he tells the bartender. She nods and steps away to grab our drinks. "What just happened?" Spencer asks.

"You asked me."

His brow furrows as he turns sideways and leans one elbow on the bar, bringing his body close to mine. "I told you I was buying this round."

I shake my head. "She asked you, and you asked me."

He reaches out and tucks a loose strand of hair behind my ear. "You're losing me here, Charlie. Why wouldn't I ask you?"

I have his full attention. His eyes aren't wandering. They're laser-focused on me. "You put me first," I say. My mind is a jumbled mess. This needs to be my last drink.

I freeze when he traces his index finger across my cheek. "I'd always put you first, Charlie."

What? Am I dreaming? Reaching down, I pinch my leg and jolt at the sting. "Not a dream," I mumble.

"Here you go." The bartender slides us our drinks, and Spencer slips her cash before I can even reach for my own.

"Thank you," I finally say when I can feel his gaze on me. Needing something to do, I turn to look around the bar. There's a couple in the corner kissing, and from here, it looks as if he's trying to eat her face. I scoff. "A four at best," I mumble.

"What's that?" Spencer asks.

*Shit. Shit. Shit.* I keep putting my foot in my mouth tonight. This is definitely my last drink. "Nothing."

He moves closer, which I didn't think would be possible. "Tell me," he says softly, and my body, the traitor, stands up and takes notice. I'm going to have to toss these panties when I get back to my room, and that pisses me off. They're one of my favorites.

I sigh, deciding that telling him is better than sitting here thinking about how the sound of his voice turns me on. It has to be the alcohol. Sure, he's always been attractive, but this is something altogether different. This... need that I suddenly feel is different.

"See that couple over there." I nod. "Red skirt. The guy has on a white sleeveless shirt," I explain.

"Got it. What about them?" He takes a casual drink of his beer, and even that is sexy. Who would have thought drinking a bottle of beer could be sexy?

"Charlie?" He places his hand on my arm. "What about them?" he asks again.

"I do this thing. It's stupid, but I've done it for years. I see two people kissing, and I rate it."

"Rate it?"

I nod. "Yeah, I mean, it's easy to see chemistry and desire, and that's important for a good kiss."

"Okay, I'm with you so far. So you rated them at a four?"

"Yep," I say, taking a small sip of my drink.

He nods as his eyes scan the room. "What about them? Back by the pool tables, silver dress."

I turn and find the couple he's talking about. "I'd say six."

"Explain the rating system to me."

"It's not really something I can explain. It's just a feeling I get when I see them together. Take the four couple. He looks like he's eating her face. That's not sexy. She's kind of just standing there, letting it happen."

"And the six couple?" he asks.

"See the way they're standing? His body is angled toward hers, and they're holding hands. They have feelings for each other."

"Then why not a higher rating?"

"No passion. It's just a kiss, but I can't feel their desire."

"Can you do that? Feel other people's desire when they kiss?"

I shrug. "Sometimes. It's more of something I can see. I know I'm weird. Just forget it."

"No." He places his beer on the bar, and his eyes bore into mine. "I want you to rate me."

"W-What? That's crazy."

"Not crazy, Charlie." He leans in close.

"Who are you going to kiss?" I ask. Is that jealousy I feel stirring in my gut?

His hand cradles the side of my face. "You."

"M-Me? No. No, not me, Spencer."

"It's just a kiss, Charlie."

"Charlotte."

He grins. "Beautiful Charlotte." He leans in a little more, our lips a breath apart. "You ready? I want you to have a clear mind for this. I'm about to show you a ten."

I scoff, and he chuckles. The sound has my heart squeezing in my chest.

"Close your eyes, Charlie."

"You're not kissing me."

"I am."

"Spencer—"

That's all I manage to get out before his lips press to mine. His lips are soft, and I can taste the beer on his breath. His hand remains on my cheek, and his thumb traces gently. I lean into him, wanting to be closer. Needing more. I don't know how long it lasts, but when he pulls back, his eyes are hooded, and I'm breathing heavily.

As far as kisses go, it was pretty PG. There was no tongue involved, but I am still breathing like I've run a marathon.

"How was that, sweet Charlotte?" he asks softly.

It takes me a few moments to process what he's asking me. "Four at best," I tell him.

He places his hand that was holding my cheek against his chest over his heart. "You wound me, woman."

I shrug as some of the fog his kiss left behind starts to clear. "Looks like you need to work on your technique," I tell him, reaching for my

drink. I slip off the stool. "Thanks for the drink." I hold up said drink, then turn on my heel and rush back to the table.

Adeline has her nose buried in her phone, Jasper and Lorelei are standing off to the side of the dance floor talking with serious looks on their faces, and Amara and Tyler are missing. At least no one seemed to notice what just happened at the bar. That's all I need, to explain to my sister's friends how I let my rival kiss me, and even worse, I enjoyed it.

"Best out of three," Spencer says, taking his seat next to mine.

"What?" I turn to look at him.

He leans in so our friends can't hear him. "I want another kiss, Charlie. Four." He shakes his head as if he can't believe I'd rank him at a four.

He's right. It was barely a kiss, and it was a solid eight, but no way will I ever tell him that. "You had your shot, big guy," I tell him.

"Charlotte," he growls, and I giggle.

Giggle.

Me.

Charlotte Krause does not giggle, and definitely not with this man. "Better luck next time." I drain the rest of my drink and place the empty glass on the table. "I need the ladies' room," I announce and stand from the table. I don't waste time moving through the crowd to the ladies' room. Once inside, I lock myself in a stall and have a mini freak-out.

Spencer Pennington kissed me.

I didn't hate it.

# Chapter SIX

 Spencer

THIS WEEK HAS BEEN DRAGGING by at a snail's pace, and it's only Wednesday. It might have something to do with the fact that my mind is still in Florida and on the Krause sisters. I've texted Audrey a few times, checking on her, and she assures me she's good.

And Charlotte, well, I can't stop thinking about her. Fucking four. That woman is maddening. My kiss was not a four. The sexy beauty doesn't know it yet, but I'm going to get a redo, and when I do, I'm going to kiss the fucking breath from her lungs.

Despite her ridiculously low rating of our kiss, there was a kiss. Damn, her lips were soft, and the way she leaned into me. I reach down to my cock and adjust myself beneath my desk. She's always done it for me, but I know all too well she'll never give me the time of day. I know she never would have let me kiss her had she not been drinking. Now, all I need to do is figure out how to get her that relaxed again, so I can get another taste.

A knock on my office door pulls me out of my thoughts. "Come in," I call out.

My administrative assistant, Cheryl, pops her head inside. "Linc is on line three."

"Take a message."

"He said if you don't take his call, he's coming to see you," she tells me.

"Bastard," I mumble under my breath. "Fine. Thank you, Cheryl." She nods and closes the door. I glare at my phone. I've been avoiding my best friend all week. We got back into town late Sunday night, and I didn't have the energy to deal with him. As the week has progressed, so has my anger. What he did to Audrey was a dick move. If he wasn't happy, he would have known before the day of their wedding. Why play games, telling her, fuck, telling all of us that he was on the road when he wasn't?

With a heavy sigh, I pick up the phone, hit the button for line three, and place the receiver next to my ear. "Asshole," I greet him.

He chuckles. "I deserve that."

"What the fuck, Linc? What happened?" I'm not hiding my irritation.

"Look, I know it was a shitty way to handle it. I'm sorry that I bailed and left you guys to handle my mess. Fuck, man, I didn't know what else to do. It just sort of hit me that Audrey and I getting married wasn't right, and it tore me up inside. I'm not used to feeling that way. Every day I work with people, and I can schmooze with the best of them, but this was Audrey, Spence." He pauses, but I remain quiet, letting him collect his thoughts. "I don't know, man. I care about her."

"You care about her? Linc, fuck, you left her on the day you were supposed to pledge to love her forever, and you care about her?"

"I love her, but it isn't the kind of love that she deserves. I realized that too late, out of the blue, and I panicked. I'm married to my job. That's who I am. She deserves someone who loves her before all else."

"Oh, so you did it for her, right? Is that what you're saying?"

"Believe it or not, yes. That doesn't excuse the way that I dealt with the situation, but I just... I shut down. It hit me out of nowhere, but then again, not really. It's been something I've thought about a lot the last few months."

"So you could have talked to her about this before we all drove to fucking Florida with your fiancée for your wedding that you failed to show up for. That's bullshit, Linc."

"I know. It sounds like a cop-out, but it's the truth. When Audrey came home Sunday night, I was there, and I knew, just by looking into her eyes, that I'd made the right decision. She agrees. Yes, I could have gone about it better. I should have mentioned my concerns to her, and I'm confident we would have had the same outcome. She agrees, but she's still processing everything. She's an amazing woman, but this life, married to a man who is married to his work, isn't what she wants."

"How kind of you to figure that out for her."

"Look, I know you're pissed. You're not the only one, but I did what I had to do. The timing was shit, but I didn't do it to be an asshole. I really do care about her, but she deserves more."

"Yeah," I agree. I don't really know what to say. It's his life, and he needs to make the choices that are best for him, but seeing the hurt in her eyes, witnessing the pain, and the heartbreak, it ripped a hole in my chest.

"I don't expect you to understand, and no offense, but it doesn't matter if you do. Audrey is the only one who needs to understand my reasoning behind why I did what I did."

"Not your best friend, or your best man, or your brother, or your friends, or your parents, or her sister, and her friends. We were all affected by this decision, Lincoln. You're going to have to give us some time to accept this new reality."

"I know that. You all also need to understand that this is my life. My future, and my choice. I never wanted to hurt her, and I do love her, just not the way she deserves to be loved."

I expel a heavy breath, close my eyes, and lean back in my chair. "It was fucking tough, man. Walking into that room and seeing the emotions play across her face. Next fucking time you ask someone to marry you, make sure it's what you want. I'm not doing this shit again."

He laughs softly, and I can feel some of my anger subside. Lincoln is a good guy, and even though I hate how he handled it, it sounds like it was a very difficult, mature decision, even if he waited too long to make it. "Deal. Now, I've been trying to call you all week. I have a favor to ask."

"What's up?"

"Audrey and I talked, and she's staying at the condo while she packs up her things. I've been staying at a hotel. You think I could crash with you for a few days until she's all moved out?"

"Sure. Where is she moving to?"

"With Charlotte."

At the sound of her name, my time with her this weekend comes rushing back. I want to tell Lincoln, and before I would have, but there's something about knowing that I tasted her lips, even with her ridiculous rating, I want to keep for just me. For us.

"Yeah, you know the code to get in the door," I tell him. I hate bulky keys in my pocket. The first thing I did when I bought my house was install keyless entry door handles. Best investment I've ever made.

"Thanks, man. I checked out of the hotel this morning. If you didn't answer, I was going to brave staying at my parents' place."

"What about Liam?" I ask.

"He's... pissed."

"Yeah, he was the one to actually say the words. It was tough, man. Give him some time."

"I know. All right. I'll see you later. Thanks, Spence."

"You're welcome. I'll see you later." Placing my receiver back on the base, I turn to stare out the window. I should be looking over the buyout of the pediatric practice the hospital is purchasing, but instead, I see a blue-eyed, red-haired angel with soft lips. I've always wondered what it would be like to kiss her. Never in my wildest dreams did I think that when I did, she would be all I thought about.

Forcing myself to get back to work, I grab the contract from my desk and start from the beginning. I didn't retain a single word when I was going over it earlier.

Hours pass as I immerse myself in my work.

A knock comes at the door, and I look up to see Cheryl standing just inside the door with a bag from what I know is the deli down the street. "You've been in here for hours." She smiles. "I picked you up something when I went out."

"You're too good to me, Cheryl," I tell her, reaching into my pocket to grab my wallet and hand her some cash.

"This is too much." She tries to give one of the ten-dollar bills back to me.

"Nope. You fly, I buy," I tell her, and she smiles.

"Thank you, Spencer."

"You're welcome. Thank you for feeding me. I've wanted to read through the final copy of this buyout contract to mark it off my list."

She nods. "I scheduled a walk-through with the practice administrator on Friday at ten in the morning."

"Thank you. The board meeting is Monday night, so that's perfect. What would I do without you?" I ask her. Her cheeks pinken. Cheryl is in her early fifties and the best fucking assistant on the planet. She's a joy to work with. She keeps me organized and fed when I don't take time to stop and eat, and I hope she never retires.

I know she will eventually, and I'll probably riot or whatever equivalent. Maybe I can bribe her to stay longer. I know we are still several years away from that happening, but she's so good that I'm already dreading the day.

I spend the last few hours of the day replying to what feels like a million emails. Finally, at five o'clock, I'm ready to call it. There are long hard days being the CEO of Charleston Memorial Hospital, a position I was lucky to grab right out of college. I'd done some interning with the previous CEO and somehow, he managed to convince the board, my young blood was exactly what they needed as his replacement. The job isn't a straight nine-to-five, but today, I'm done. I want to go home, strip out of this suit, grab a shower, some food, and maybe a cold beer, and catch up with Linc before crashing into my California king.

I'm sitting on the couch with my feet propped up. I just finished dinner, just a couple of burgers on the grill, and now I'm relaxing with a cold beer. The front door opens, and I turn to look over my shoulder to see Lincoln stepping inside with a duffel bag thrown over his shoulder.

"Hey, man," he says hesitantly.

"I'm not really feeling up to throwing hands tonight," I tell him with a chuckle. His shoulders relax.

"I wouldn't fight back if you were," he says. He drops his duffel bag to the floor and plops down in the recliner. "It was the right thing to do, but I still feel like shit."

I ignore his comment. "There are a couple of burgers on the counter if you're hungry."

"Yeah, that'd be great."

"You just getting off work?" I ask. Glancing at the clock on the wall, I see it's after seven.

He shrugs. "This is an early night for me."

I finish off my beer and stand. "The spare bedroom is yours. I'm going to shower and call it a night."

"It's not even eight." I hear the surprise in his voice.

"I need my beauty sleep. I don't stay this handsome naturally." I laugh.

"Fuck off." He chuckles. "Thanks, man, for letting me stay here."

I nod. "You're my best friend. I might not agree with the way you handled the situation, but that doesn't mean I hate you. Pissed off, yeah, but that's diminishing slowly. Just do better." I feel like my father lecturing him. "You know where everything is," I say.

He holds his fist out for me, and I knock my knuckles against his before taking my now-empty bottle of beer to the recycling bin and heading upstairs to shower. By the time I reach my bedroom door, my shirt is off, and I toss it on the chair in the corner, along with the others from this week. My suit jacket is still downstairs. I make a mental note to grab it all Friday morning and drop them off at the dry cleaners before my meeting with the pediatric practice we're buying.

We just renovated our maternity ward, and adding pediatrics to our list of available services is a good move. For all the babies we deliver, we can refer to our own pediatricians, and they'll do rounds on all newborns. I went back and forth with the board, trying to decide if we should build an office and hire new physicians or buy an existing local practice. I guess word got around because three weeks ago, Dr. Phillips called and said that he and his partners were interested in selling.

I jumped at the opportunity, and the board agreed. The contract is ready, and the last step is for me to tour the facility and meet the physicians and staff. This deal has been in the works for months. I've already looked at the numbers, and the practice is profitable. Our CFO has signed off on the numbers as well. I'm just triple-checking at this point. I'm a young CEO and I don't want to make a huge mistake that will hinder the hospital in any way. The physicians are all equal partners, and they're tired of the business side of things. They just want to see their patients and be done. It's the perfect scenario for all of us. It also helps that they're located just a few blocks from the hospital.

Quickly discarding the rest of my clothes and tossing the dry-cleaning items on the chair, I throw the rest in the hamper in the corner. My bathroom is one of the reasons I bought this house. The shower is huge. Walk-in, with a long bench in the corner. There isn't a shower door and no curtain to deal with. When I turn the water on, the rain shower head starts, as well as the jets. They're extra, and I didn't think I'd ever use them, but damn, they're nice after a long-ass day sitting at my desk looking over contracts. They, combined with the scorching-hot water, help soothe my sore muscles.

Steam quickly fills the room, and I step under the hot spray. Dipping my head, I let the water rain down on the back of my neck as the stress of the day washes away. Instantly, Charlotte and her soft lips pop into my mind. I can't escape her. My cock thickens just thinking about her gorgeous auburn hair and those crystal-blue eyes.

It's not the first time, and it surely won't be the last, that I palm my cock and slide my hand from root to tip with thoughts of her. It doesn't matter what woman I'm with or who I meet. Every single fucking time my rosy palm meets my cock, it's Charlotte that I think about. Ten years of jacking my cock to her, and finally, I've tasted her, and now I can't go twenty-four hours without rubbing one out.

Leaning my head against the tile wall, I brace my hand there and allow myself to get lost in the fantasy of Charlotte. Tonight, she's sitting on my desk, legs spread wide, her bare pussy on display for me. I'm sitting in my chair, having her for lunch. Her kisses are soft and sweet, and I can only imagine that her pussy is even better. Of course it is. This is Charlotte Krause we're talking about.

I groan as my fist pumps faster. I imagine her hands buried in my hair, legs locked tight around my neck as I devour her, pulling every ounce of pleasure from her body as I drown in her orgasm.

"Fuck," I grunt as my orgasm crashes over me. It's intense, and I'm breathing heavily as I imagine her blue eyes staring down at me, sated and full of desire, only for me. I give myself a few minutes to live in my fantasy before standing and quickly showering.

After toweling off, I slide into a pair of boxer briefs, plug my phone in to charge on the nightstand, and glide beneath the covers. I used to see Charlotte when I would visit Lincoln and Audrey. Now, I don't know how, but I'm going to find a way to see her. I have to kiss her again.

No, I need to.

Not just to show her that her rating of a four was ridiculous but because even the small pieces of her that I get are better than never getting to see her.

I don't want to know what a world without Charlotte Krause in my life is like.

# Chapter SEVEN

## Charlotte

As soon as I walk into the building, I see Dr. Phillips standing outside of my office. "Good morning," I greet him as I draw closer.

"Morning, Charlotte." He beams. "You have a few minutes?"

"Absolutely." I step into my office, flip on the light, place my purse on the credenza behind my desk, and turn to face him. "What's up?"

"Remember how I had you move my patients for this afternoon to yesterday, which was my day off?"

I nod. "I do. Did your plans fall through, and you want to be put back on the schedule today for acute visits?"

"No. I still have a meeting today, and I want you to be there."

"Sure. Is there anything you need me to prepare beforehand?"

"You've already done it. Over the last few weeks, all the reports I've had you run."

"Okay. Well, just tell me when and where." I grin at him even though I feel a little uneasy.

"I didn't tell you sooner because I don't want word to get out to the staff until everything is finalized."

"May I ask what the meeting is about?"

"A buyout."

I freeze. "Buyout? Our numbers are great." I'm floored that he and the other partners are even considering this.

He nods. "They are, but the partners and I discussed it, and we're not business-minded people. We just want to see our patients and forget about RVUs, EHRs, JCAHO, and all the other things we have to deal with."

"That's why you have me." I smile, even though it's forced.

"This has nothing to do with you or your ability to run this place. Ultimately, it rests on our shoulders as the owners, and we're ready to let that piece go."

"So, what happens?"

"We have it written into the contract that all current staff stays in place. We do have to switch over to their human resources policies, but I've looked them over, and ours are very similar. No one loses their job unless they do something in violation of those rules and regulations."

"You're still going to have to deal with all the things you listed off."

He nods. "I know, but only from the medical side, not the business side. The partners have been talking about this for months. We heard of a local facility looking to add pediatrics to their roster, and I reached out. They'll be here this morning at ten. They want to meet you and tour all three offices."

"I'll be here for this one, as it's our main location. I'd like for you to take them to both satellite locations this afternoon. Give them full access to any information they ask for, and don't hold anything back."

I nod slowly. "I can do that."

"Thank you, Charlotte. I'm sorry for dropping this on you like this, but again, I don't want the staff to know what's going on. I don't want them to worry."

"I understand. Who are we meeting with today?" I ask.

THE *Kissing* GAMES

"I'm not certain how many people will be here. I'm hoping it's a small group so that the staff isn't as curious. However, we'll deal with that as it happens. This is the final piece. If they like what they see today, they're going to sign the contract. We signed last night. I don't anticipate any issues today."

"Okay. Well, I better get to work. I'll be ready at ten when they're here. Should I order pastries or lunch, maybe?"

"I took care of having lunch catered. It's been a while since we treated the staff, and then we'll set up for a private lunch with our guests in the conference room. It will just be you and me. The other providers have full patient loads."

"All right. Well, if anything changes between now and then, let me know." My smile is forced, but I'm hoping it's not obvious. I know he said that all of our jobs are safe, but a buyout always changes things. I love this job, my staff, and the physicians. This is not what I needed on top of last week's drama.

Speaking of, I make a mental note to check and see if we have any boxes that I can drop off to Audrey. She's been packing up her things this week while Lincoln is staying at a hotel or maybe with Liam, I assume. She's going to be staying with me for a while until she gets on her feet. I'd never tell her this because I don't want her to think that I'm happy that her wedding never happened, but I'm excited to have her staying with me.

By the time I graduated with my master's, Audrey was in college too. I've been living on my own, and while I enjoy my space, it will be nice to have her here. It won't be so lonely for a change.

Taking a seat at my desk, I fire up my computer and get busy. My day just got high-jacked. I spend the next two hours multi-tasking, wearing eight million hats as I do on any given day. As practice administrator of a privately owned practice, I'm accounting, maintenance, human resources, IT, and anything and everything else that happens to arise that needs to be taken care of. It keeps me busy, but I love it. I couldn't imagine doing anything different with my life.

Well, that's not true either. I'd love to be a mom, but you have to fall in love for that to happen, or at least be dating. Sure, I know there are other ways, but my best-kept secret is that I want the fairy tale. My parents were so in love with each other. I want that.

I want a man who looks at me as if I'm the best gift he's ever received, and I want to be the woman who stands by his side, supporting him through life.

A quick glance at the clock shows me it's a few minutes before our guests are due to arrive. I dash down the hall for a quick bathroom break before making my way to the conference room. I walk around, pushing in chairs and tossing a leftover napkin from where one of the physicians must have eaten lunch in here earlier this week. The room is ready, but my nerves are not. I'm not a fan of change. I've had enough change in my lifetime. But Dr. Phillips seemed excited and confident that this buyout is what's best for everyone.

I just hope he's right.

I hear voices down the hall. I stand up straight and smooth out the black pencil skirt and white, flowing top I'm wearing today. I plaster a smile on my face, and as soon as Dr. Phillips steps into the room, I see who he's with, and my smile drops.

"Mr. Pennington, this is our practice administrator—"

"Charlie. I mean Charlotte," Spencer corrects. A slow, sexy grin tugs at his lips. He studies me for several long heartbeats before offering Dr. Phillips more information. "We went to college together." He steps toward me and offers me his hand. "Good to see you again." He's not once taken his eyes off me since he walked through the door.

My heart pounds in my chest. What in the hell is he doing here? I wipe my sweaty palms on my skirt as my mind races with what I know about Spencer. Suddenly everything clicks. He's the CEO of our local hospital, Charleston Memorial, and he's going to be my new boss if this plan goes through. He tilts his head to the side, and I realize his hand is still suspended in the air. "You too," I say, taking his hand. There's a tremor in my voice because I'm freaking the hell out. This can't be happening. He gently traces his thumb over mine before he releases his hold, which lasts far longer than a greeting handshake should have.

"I didn't realize you two knew each other, but that will make today that much easier. Charlotte will be escorting you to our two satellite locations," Dr. Phillips explains. Spencer pulls his searing gaze from mine and gives Dr. Phillips his attention. "She knows our facilities and operations like the back of her hand, so you'll be in good hands," Dr. Phillips explains.

Spencer looks over at me, and his brown eyes smolder. "I'm certain her hands will be just fine," he replies.

"Great." Dr. Phillips claps his hands.

How did he miss that innuendo? How do I get out of this? It hits me that I'm going to have to look for a new job. No way I can work under him. An image of me physically under him pops into my mind, but I push it down. Way, way down deep. Our previous weekend together has me out of sorts. I don't think about Spencer like that. That's not who we are, but those eyes of his, the dark orbs, seem to be undressing me on their own accord. I shift on my feet, feeling uncomfortable under his gaze. Reaching out, I grip the leather chair in front of me.

"Let's get started. We have about an hour and a half before lunch is delivered, and then the two of you can head to the satellite offices." Dr. Phillips pulls out a chair and takes a seat. He has no idea my heart is about to beat out of my chest or that if my hand wasn't gripping the back of the chair in front of me, I might crumple to the floor because my knees are shaking so badly.

"Dr. Phillips—" I lick my suddenly dry lips. "I'd love for you to join us." My tone is even, and I don't know how I'm pulling it off because I'm shaking on the inside. My world has just been turned upside down with this new information. It's bad enough I didn't know about the potential buyout until this morning, and now this. Spencer Pennington, my college rival and a royal pain in my ass, is going to be my new boss.

I have to find a new job.

Sadness washes over me. I love what I do. I love the physicians and the staff, but there is no way in hell that Spencer is going to be my boss. I'll deal until I find something new, but I'm definitely going to start my search.

Why can nothing ever be easy? I feel like Audrey and I, since losing our parents, have been running a rat race that never seems to slow down.

"You'll do just fine, Charlotte," he says kindly. "Now, let's get down to it. Mr. Pennington, what questions do you have for us?"

Spencer begins to ask questions about the processes of the practice, new patient acquisition, and staffing. I don't know how, but I manage to answer questions when they're directed at me, but for the most part, I let Dr. Phillips take the lead. It pisses me off because the last thing I want is for Spencer to think that I'm shit at my job.

I'm not.

I'm damn good at what I do, but I've been thrown a huge curveball today, and I'm struggling to make sense of it all. I hate that I'm going to have to find a new job, and then there's the worry that I won't find anything in Charleston. Audrey just moved in with me, and I can't abandon her, not after what she's been through. I'm just going to have to suck it up and deal. I mean, how involved will he be? Surely, he has a COO or director that will handle the day-to-day. What CEO works directly with a practice administrator? I'm freaking out because it's him.

Everything is going to work out.

I hope.

"Well, lunch should be here." Dr. Phillips stands, and I realize we've been in this room for close to two hours talking, and I didn't retain one single thing we discussed. I need to get it together. "Charlotte, I'll leave you with Mr. Pennington. Enjoy lunch and the rest of your day. Mr. Pennington." He turns to look at Spencer. "If you have any additional questions after seeing the other two locations, please let me know."

"Thank you, Dr. Phillips." Spencer stands and shakes his hand. "I'll be in touch."

Dr. Phillips nods, and then it's just the two of us.

"Small world, huh?" Spencer asks.

"I don't suppose I could talk you out of this deal?" I ask him.

He chuckles. "It's a good business move for me. Why would I do that?"

"This can't be happening," I mutter under my breath. Pushing back from the table, I stand and move toward the door. "If you're hungry, follow me."

"Is that any way to treat your new boss?" Spencer asks. His long legs close the distance between us. He doesn't stop until he's toe to toe with me.

THE *Kissing* GAMES

I tilt my head back to look at him. "You're not my boss yet."

My breath hitches when he bends over, leaning in close and placing his lips next to my ear. "This is happening, Charlie." He stands back to his full height. "Get used to seeing me around." He smiles, and even though he has a beard, I know there is a dimple hiding in there, and I hate that. I wish that I could see it.

"Don't worry. I'll be looking for new employment as soon as this day ends." I turn back to the door and immediately feel his hand at my elbow before I can pull it open.

"Charlotte," he says softly. I don't turn to look at him. My emotions are all over the place, and hot tears prick my eyes. His thumb rubs circles on my arm where he's still keeping me from leaving the room. His grip is loose but still effective. "Look at me."

"Can we not do this, Spencer? Please?" My voice cracks. I swallow hard. "Not here."

What happens next has my knees turning to jelly, and I'm glad he has a hold on me and that I have a hold on the door handle. Because when he leans in close, his scent surrounding me, and presses his lips to my temple, I barely stay up on my feet.

The feel of his soft lips against my skin, the heat of his touch, it's all too much. I have to get out of this room. I need some space, just a damn minute to breathe and process that my afternoon will be spent with him.

He drops his hand, and I take a moment to take in a long deep breath and slowly exhale before pulling open the door, plastering a smile on my face, and leading him to the break room to make himself a plate.

Thankfully, the staff still have ten minutes before we turn the phones off for lunch, so Spencer and I are able to make our plates before without anyone watching us. I'm grateful because I know the tension between us is palpable. I feel it as though it's a living, breathing thing stretched between us, and that is not something my staff needs to see.

Once we both have our plates made, I lead him back to the conference room, where I shut the door. Not because I want to be alone with him but because I don't want prying eyes to see how uncomfortable I am.

"How has your week been?" Spencer asks.

I look up at him just as I am about to take a bite of my turkey sub on wheat. "Do you really care?"

He chuckles. "Do I look like a man that would ask a question he doesn't care to know the answer to?"

"Are you forgetting that I know the pre-CEO Spencer? The one who walked around the Clemson campus as if he owned the world? The same guy who could smile, and the ladies would practically toss their panties at you. Or the guy that would gloat if he got a higher grade than me? I know that guy, and he doesn't give a fuck how my week has been."

"Charlie—"

"Mr. Pennington, my name is Charlotte." I avoid his gaze and choose to stare down at my plate as if it's the most interesting thing I've seen in my entire existence. I can't look at him. Those dark brown eyes will be assessing me, and he'll see too much. He'll see that I wanted those smiles directed at me, that I wanted to talk about our grades and mutual classes, not compete. He's been my rival for as long as I can remember, but deep down, that's not what I wanted us to be. That's just... who we were, and I've accepted that. That's all we ever will be. Well, until a few hours ago when I found out Spencer Pennington is no longer just my college rival. He's my new boss.

# Chapter EIGHT

*Spencer*

SHE'S IGNORING ME WHILE SHE picks at her food. I know this because I can't take my eyes off her. I've sifted through every conversation I've ever had with Dr. Phillips and all the documentation that I've read about this practice, and never once did her name come up.

Not once.

Dr. Phillips always refers to her as their practice administrator, and her name isn't listed on their website and, of course, on none of their financials. I knew that she also worked in healthcare. I just didn't know in what capacity. I feel as though I've been duped, but I'm the only one to blame here. I should have done more research. Fuck, I should have asked her where she was working. I've had plenty of chances over the years, but I spend my time verbally sparring with her instead of asking the important questions. No wonder she shot my ass down all those years ago.

"How long have you worked here?" I ask to kill the void of silence that stretches between us.

"First job after grad school." Her tone is clipped, and it pisses me off.

"Me too, thanks for asking," I snark back at her.

"Didn't ask, don't care."

"Is that how you speak to your boss?" I taunt. Her shoulders stiffen, and I know that I've struck a nerve. Fuck, why do I always have to be an ass where she's concerned?

"You're not my boss yet."

"But I will be. All that's standing between making that happen is my signature on the contract in my briefcase."

She shrugs. "Won't be for long."

"Oh? Dr. Phillips didn't tell me that you were leaving." The thought that she's changing jobs doesn't sit well with me.

"I wasn't until a few hours ago." She lifts her eyes to mine and meets my stare head-on.

"You're leaving because of the buyout?" I ask, but I don't need confirmation. The answer is written all over her face.

"Is that a real question?" she sasses.

Before I get the chance to reply, the door to the conference room opens, and in steps Dr. Phillips. "Good, the two of you have had lunch. Mr. Pennington, I look forward to hearing from you after you've toured the other locations." He gives me a kind smile before turning his gaze to Charlotte. "Charlotte, Mr. Pennington is to have full access to anything regarding the practice. You two be safe, and let me know if there is anything else you might need." With a nod, he leaves just as quickly as he entered, closing the door softly behind him.

"Are you done?" Charlotte asks, nodding to my half-eaten sandwich.

"Are you?" I raise my eyebrows in question, and we both know I'm not asking if she's finished with her food.

"I'm working on it." She stands and gathers her trash, tossing it into the can next to the door. "I need to grab my things. I'll be right back." She pulls open the door and rushes down the hall, and no way am I sitting here waiting for her.

I'm on my feet, tossing my lunch in the can with hers and following her down the hall. When I reach her office door, I pause and watch her. She has both hands braced on her desk, and her head is bowed, but I can tell by the rise and fall of her shoulders, she's breathing heavily. My eyes scan the room, and I smile when I see a picture of her and Audrey on the bookshelf at what looks like Charlotte's college graduation.

Not willing to take my eyes off her for too long, I turn my gaze back to the woman in front of me. "I'll drive." It's lame, but the best that I've got. If I try to say anything to make this better for her, I'm going to end up pulling her into my arms, and I wouldn't give a single fuck who in this office sees me do it. It's best if I steer clear for now.

"You can follow me." She stands to her full height and squares her shoulders as if she's ready for a fight.

"That's ridiculous. Why should we take both cars? It's better for the environment if we only take one."

"Then I'm driving."

"Nope." I take a step into her office. "Maybe we should call Dr. Phillips and get his take on the matter. I'm sure he'll see things my way."

She opens her mouth to reply, and I'm sure, fire back at me but quickly closes it. "Whatever. Can we just go so that we can get this day over with?"

"After you." I step back and motion for her to lead the way out of her office. Once she's next to me, I place my hand at the base of her spine, and she immediately stiffens. "Just being a gentleman," I whisper just for her.

"Right," she scoffs.

Plastering a smile on my face, I try not to make eye contact with any of the staff as I lead her out to my SUV.

I pull open the passenger door for her and wait for her to climb inside. She quickly fastens her seat belt as if she's worried I might crash us before we get there. If she only knew that I consider her to be precious cargo, so I'll be extra careful with her sitting next to me.

"Do you know where we're going?" she asks once I take my seat behind the wheel.

"Yeah. I know the other locations. Which one do you want to go to first?"

"Calloway. It's the furthest away. We can work our way back to Bridgewater and then back to the main office in Charleston."

She crosses her arms over her chest and immediately turns to look out the window instead of at me. Her body language tells me that she wants to be anywhere but here, but there is a sparkle in her eyes that tells another story.

I need to see that sparkle.

"Charlie?" I wait for her to turn to look at me, but she doesn't. This calls for drastic measures. Reaching over, I place my hand on her thigh. Her skirt is tight over her thighs where she sits, and my hand rests perfectly. "Look at me." I wait. Her eyes move to my hand on her thigh before slowly rising to mine. "There she is." I smile at her.

"You shouldn't be touching me. That's sexual harassment." Her words tell me to stop, but her sparkling eyes tell me she likes it.

"Do you want me to move my hand, Charlie?"

"I— Yes, you should."

"I didn't ask you if you thought that I should." I turn in my seat to get a better look at her. My body is angled toward hers as much as the seat will allow. "I asked you if you wanted me to move my hand."

"I am your employee."

"Not yet," I counter. "Tell me, Charlie."

She nods, not able to give me the words, so I lift my hand from her thigh, already missing the contact even through her skirt. The need to feel her skin against mine is so strong that I take the same hand and mold it to her cheek. "You should let me kiss you." My voice is husky even to my own ears.

"W-What?" she stammers.

I keep my eyes locked on hers. "I want to kiss you."

"You want to kiss me?" She repeats my words as if she doesn't understand the meaning of them.

THE *Kissing* GAMES

"More than anything," I say, knowing I'm giving her too much. I don't know why, but after last weekend, the me that used to be an asshole to her just doesn't seem to fit us. Not anymore. I've tasted her, and spent time with her, where she started to let her guard down and it's led me to wonder if I wasn't wrong all those years ago. I thought she shot me down because she felt like she was better than me, but that doesn't seem to be who she is.

My head is a mess over this woman, and I can't stop thinking about kissing her. A fucking four, really? I can do better, and I'm damn well going to prove that to her.

"I don't think that's a good idea," she replies with a hushed whisper.

That's not a no. "Maybe we should try it and see?"

"Spencer." She sighs.

"Just one, Charlie."

"We're in the parking lot of my work. The office your hospital is trying to buy. This isn't a good plan."

I nod and sit back in my seat, adjusting my seat belt around my chest and locking it in place before starting my SUV and pulling out of the lot. I drive one block, turn right into the pharmacy parking lot, and put the SUV in Park. Unclasping my seat belt, I turn to face her. My hand goes back to her cheek, and she tilts her head just slightly. If I wasn't watching her as closely as I am, I would have missed it.

"What are you doing?" she asks softly.

"Fixing the problem. Now we're just in a random parking lot."

"In the middle of the day."

"Is there a rule about kissing in the middle of the day?" My lips quirk up in a smile. I can't seem to help myself where Charlotte is concerned.

"No. No kissing."

"Just one. Come on. You have to give me a chance to up my score." I watch as she bites down on her lip to keep from smiling.

"Four at best, Pennington," she razzes.

I lean in close, our lips barely a breath apart. "I can do better." I hover, our breath mingling, but I don't move any closer. "Tell me I can kiss you, Charlie."

She rolls those big blue eyes. "Fine. If it will get you to stop asking. It's pointless," she says, her voice a breathy whisper.

"What's pointless?"

"You trying to up your number? You're a four, Spencer. It's okay. I knew there was something you weren't perfect at. I just never thought it would be this."

The words are barely out of her mouth before I press my lips to hers. Hers are just as soft as I remember them being. It's not even been a full week since I last kissed her, yet her taste still seems new.

As I slide my tongue across her lips, she opens for me, just like I need her to, and I dip my tongue inside. Her hands grip my shirt as she sucks on my tongue, taking over what's supposed to be my kiss. Not that I'm complaining. I'm expecting a low rating because that's the game she wants to play, and I'm fine with that. It just gives me more motivation to convince her to kiss me again, to test out my rating again.

I can play this kissing game as long as she's willing. It's not a hardship to kiss the beauty sitting in my passenger seat, gripping my shirt like she's afraid I might disappear at any moment.

My hand slides behind her neck, allowing me to pull her closer, to hold her lips to mine. Fuck, I could get lost in this woman and not give a single fuck if I ever came up for air again. The honking of a horn off in the distance causes her to freeze and pull away. I don't let her get far, instead holding her close and resting my forehead against hers.

"Well?" I ask, trying to catch my breath.

"I guess that was a little better," she mumbles. Her eyes are closed, and her lips are red and swollen.

It takes every ounce of willpower I have not to kiss her again. "I need a number, Charlie."

"Four."

"No way, babe. That was not a four." Softly, I run the pad of my thumb over the pulse in her neck. "Does a four make your pulse race?" I ask, my voice low. "Does a four make your pussy ache?" I ask when I see her shifting in her seat.

"Spencer!" she scolds.

THE *Kissing* GAMES

"Tell me, Charlie. If I were to slide my hand between your thighs, under that sexy-as-fuck skirt you're wearing, would I find you wet and wanting me?" My cock presses against the zipper of my pants, but that doesn't stop me. I'm just making this worse on myself, thinking about her pussy being swollen and wet, needing me to take the ache away.

Me.

She's wet for me.

I don't need to see it. Her eyes tell me everything that I need to know. "So tell me again, what's my number?" I ask, my lips grazing her ear.

"F-Five."

A deep chuckle pulls from my chest. I place a kiss on her temple and sit back in my seat. "We both know that was not a five, but I like this kissing game we're playing. Gives me more chances to kiss you."

"What? No. No games. You are not going to kiss me again. This was— No. Not anymore, Spencer. We can't."

"We can and we will." I want to lean over this console and fucking devour her lips, but I refrain. I'm learning so much about this woman. She's not at all who I thought she was, and my need to learn everything about her is deep-rooted. Almost as much as I want her to admit that my kisses rock her world.

Putting the SUV in Drive, I pull out of the parking spot and back out onto the road. The drive to Calloway is quiet, just the soft hum of the radio in the background. It's so low I can't make out the lyrics, but that's okay. I like the fact that we're riding together and we're not arguing for once.

Truth be told, I argue with her to get her attention. She dismissed me so easily, as if I was nothing. That's the only way I knew to get her attention. It pissed her off, then we started competing for grades, and ten years later, here we are. I never imagined she would be back in my life like this. First, as the sister of the woman my best friend was going to marry. Now, as my future employee.

All week I've thought of her constantly, and this morning she was there as if just thinking about her brought her back into my everyday world. I didn't know how I was going to see her again, and now here she is. Sitting next to me. Spending time with me. That's when an idea hits me. I can drag this out. I can request more information, tell the physicians that the board needs to look at the numbers again, something, anything, to keep her with me like this.

Maybe, just maybe, in time, she'll be okay with kissing her rival. Who knows, maybe there is more for us than this game we're playing. What I do know is that I'm going to make it so that we have the time to figure it out.

# Chapter NINE

## Charlotte

"THIS IS OUR SECOND LARGEST location," I tell Spencer as we walk through the halls of the Calloway practice. I've already pointed out the exam rooms, physicians' offices, and break room. "And this is the meeting room. It's not as large as the one we have back in Charleston." I keep my voice professional and devoid of emotion.

I'm very aware of his tall frame next to me. I can feel the heat of his body as his shoulder brushes against mine, but I keep my expression neutral. I refuse to let him see that I'm not as immune to him as I pretend to be.

"How many exam rooms again?" he asks.

"Nine. We usually have up to three physicians each day at this location, depending on vacation schedules and things like that."

He nods. "How are the numbers as far as visits are concerned?"

I know that he already has this information, but he's talking about work, and that's something that I can focus on. I know my job like the back of my hand. This is a good neutral conversation. "Great. We fill every day. We save about thirty percent of our daily visits for acute appointments, and those always fill." Pushing open the door to the small meeting room, I stand back, letting him pass. His shoulder brushes against my chest as he steps into the room, and I feel that simple graze all the way to the tips of my toes. I knew I should have stepped back, but the sinister part of me, the part that doesn't despise Spencer as much as I claim to, wanted to feel his body rub against mine, no matter how brief the contact was.

He takes a seat at the small table, and I need to put space between us, so I take the one directly across from him. Not that it keeps my traitorous body from wanting to be close to him, but my mind knows we need to stay away.

"Do you know the percentage of patients that are newborns? What is your policy for new patients and scheduling in new babies from existing families?" he asks, resting his hands on the table.

My eyes move to his wrists that peek out beneath his long-sleeve black button-up. The tattoos that I know cover his entire arms peek through. For a brief moment, I imagine tracing each line of ink with my tongue. A throat clears, and I shake out of my thoughts. My gaze snaps to Spencer's, who's looking at me like he might devour me.

"Newborns," I say, trying to get my mind out of the gutter and back on business. Business is safe. "Yes, we like to see breastfed babies within three days of their release from the hospital and bottle-fed babies within five days."

"New and existing families?" he asks again.

I nod. "We are open to new patients as long as we accept their insurance."

"That's good. Can you get me a list of plans your physicians are currently credentialed under? We'll need to make sure they all have privileges at our facility for rounds, but we have a team that can help expedite that process with the credentials committee."

I swallow hard. "So, this is happening?"

He studies me for several long heartbeats before he answers. "I have no concerns yet, but I'll need to see more. It's my job to do my due diligence before this deal goes through. It will be my name on the buyout, and if I'm to answer to the board for my final decision, I want to ensure that I know your operations inside and out."

"Dr. Phillips said you are to have full access to whatever you need to make this deal happen." I hold my head high, feeling confident in my ability to block out my past with the man sitting across from me.

"That's good. I'll be sure to speak to him as well to let him know that I'll be taking up some of your time in the coming weeks."

My mouth falls open, and my shoulders stiffen at his words. My belly drops to my toes. "W-What?" I manage to ask.

Those piercing brown eyes hold me captive. "I'm going to need you to assist me with processes, procedures, and reports. I'm sure Dr. Phillips will approve it."

"He said after today, it was a done deal. That the partners had signed, it was the last portion before you signed, and the deal was done." My heart begins to race as I digest his words. From the sounds of it, I'll be working closely with him for the next few weeks.

"That is the last piece, but this is on me, Charlie." His voice softens when he uses the nickname I've repeatedly asked him not to use. If I'm being honest, I've never hated him calling me Charlie. Not really. Scolding him was a way to keep him at bay. He was crude in the beginning. Well, he was after our first meeting. But now, he's different. Not at all what I expected.

"What do you need to make this happen?" My voice is gritty as I ask the question.

"Time with you." My eyes widen, and he pushes on. "Dr. Phillips assured me that you know the practice inside and out. I didn't get where I am today by making rash decisions. This is a huge acquisition for the hospital, and even though the board approved the purchase, it's because I encouraged it. I'm simply using some extra time to ensure I have all the data that I need to make an informed decision."

I slowly nod because I understand. If I were him, I would do the same thing. "All right," I concede. "I'll do whatever you need me to do."

Those chocolate eyes of his flame with something that looks a lot like desire at my words. "How about we head to the Bridgewater location?" he suggests.

THE *Kissing* GAMES

"Of course. I'll meet you outside. I just want to say goodbye to the physicians and staff."

"I'll join you." He stands and moves toward the door, waiting for me to reach him. "After you," he says and places his hand on the small of my back, leading me out of the meeting room.

His touch burns through my blouse, but I ignore the heat and the tingles that his touch creates. Instead, I quicken my pace to walk ahead of him, causing him to drop his hand. I stop by the front desk and the nurses' station before checking in with the two physicians we have here today to say goodbye.

Quietly, Spencer and I make our way out of the building and to his car. He opens the door for me, and I offer him a small smile before sliding inside. When he slides behind the wheel and buckles up, his strong hands grip the wheel, and I have to avert my gaze. Why is everything he does suddenly sexy as hell?

Staring out the passenger-side window, I think about how the next few weeks are going to go. I'm going to have to work closely with him. Maybe, if I'm lucky, I can email him what he needs, and our face-to-face interactions will be limited. A girl can dream.

We turn, and it's not toward the road that will take us to the Bridgewater location. I angle to look at Spencer. "Where are we going?"

"Oh, I thought we could grab a shake." He expertly maneuvers us into the parking lot of the local fast-food joint and pulls up to the window. "What do you want?" he asks.

"I'm okay. Thank you, though," I say politely.

His lips curl up in a smile that I lose sight of when the speaker cracks to life, the person on the other end asking if he's ready to order.

"Hi, I'll have a medium chocolate shake and a medium strawberry shake," he orders.

The lady behind the speaker rattles off a total, and he pulls up in the line. "Can you really drink two medium shakes?" I ask.

"One is for you."

"What?" I ask, stunned. "I told you I didn't want anything. Besides, what if you ordered flavors I don't like?"

"I didn't," he says confidently.

I don't really know what to say to that because he's right. Strawberry milkshakes are my favorite, but how would he know that? Did we talk about it while we were at the resort? I let all the moments with him over the three days we were there filter through my mind, and I don't recall that particular conversation.

He passes over some cash before taking the two shakes and placing them into the cupholder. The strawberry shake is on my side. He hands me a straw with a grin as he rolls up his window and pulls out of the lot. "That's your favorite, right?" he asks, turning again in the opposite direction of where we should be heading.

"How did you know?"

He pulls into the lot of the automatic car wash and waits his turn to pay the attendant. Once he hands over a ten-dollar bill, he unwraps his straw, places it in his shake, and takes a hefty pull. I've yet to touch mine, not because I'm being stubborn. Okay, maybe I'm being a little stubborn, but more so, I can't figure out how in the hell he knew that strawberry was my favorite.

"Spencer?"

He places his shake back into the cupholder and turns to look at me while we wait our turn. "I've known you for ten years, Charlie. I'm observant."

"What's Linc's favorite?"

He shrugs. "Don't know."

I'm not sure what to say to that. I'm floored that between the competition between us in college, him asking me out, and me always shooting him down, he was paying attention to more than just wanting to top my grades or add me as a mark to his bedpost.

He creeps ahead and puts the car in Neutral when the attendant tells him to. He settles back in his seat and turns his head to face me. I feel his gaze and angle my eyes to his. I know I should look away, but I can't. There's something in his stare that holds me captive.

"I can do better," he says, his voice low and gravelly.

"Better at what? Remembering my favorite shake?" I raise my brows, letting him see my confusion.

I still when he reaches up and rests his palm against my cheek. The car lurches forward, and we're surrounded and secluded, and it's suddenly way more intimate than what an automatic car wash should be.

"You rated me a four and a five, Charlie." He gives me a look that tells me he's on to my bullshit, but I hold strong with my rating and my lie.

I shrug, but his hand remains on my cheek. "Just keeping it real, Pennington."

He turns in his seat and leans over the console. "I think you should give me a chance to redeem myself." His attention moves to my lips.

"Redeem yourself?" I ask, because I'm kind of freaking out on the inside. Today has been weird. I'm obviously not immune to him, not with the way my body has been reacting to being near him and our kiss…. We might have been drinking, but I remember it. Every single second of time that his lips were pressed to mine, I remember. I chalked it up to the alcohol and the emotions of the weekend.

I don't have that excuse today.

"Spencer—" I start, but the car stops moving. A buzzer sounds, and he grins.

"Looks like someone is watching out for me."

"Because we're stuck in an automatic car wash?"

He leans in close. "Because I have more time." His eyes hold mine. "Perfection shouldn't be rushed, Charlie."

I find myself nodding in agreement, but Spencer takes that as my willingness to give him another shot to show me his kissing skills. He closes the small distance between us and presses his lips to mine.

Neither one of us moves at first, as we savor the feel of our lips pressing firmly together. My heart thunders in my chest, and I'm thankful for the loud machine surrounding us, hopeful he can't hear the rapid beat. I'm ready to pull back when he slides his hand behind my neck and traces my lips with his tongue. I gasp, not expecting that move, and he slides his tongue smoothly past my lips, where it dances with mine.

I should stop this. I should pull back and tell him he's a five at best, but that would be yet another lie. The truth is that Spencer

THE *Kissing* GAMES

Pennington is making love to my mouth right here in his car while sitting still in an automatic car wash. This is hands-down the best kiss of my entire life.

I'm kissing my rival.

And it's turning my world upside down.

I make a mewling sound from somewhere in the back of my throat, and I know I should be embarrassed, and I'm sure I will be, just not right this moment. Not while he's kissing me as if this might be the last kiss he ever gives or receives.

The hand on the back of my neck adjusts me so that my head is tilted, and he leans in closer. His body heat wraps around me, and I would never admit this out loud, but I could sit here in this car, kissing him like this every day of forever. So, yeah, if you were wondering, I'm kissing him back. I can't *not* kiss him back.

The car jerks as we once again start to move forward, and Spencer slows the kiss. When he finally pulls his mouth from mine, his eyes are so dark they almost appear to be black instead of the sparkling chocolate brown that I'm used to.

I part my lips to say something, anything, but I can't seem to form a single word. Instead, I focus on deep, even breaths, even though my chest is now rising faster than it was when we pulled into this tunnel.

Spencer watches me, and I'm about to tell him he should look out in front of him. We have to be about done with this when his low, rumbled words fill the space around us. "So. Fucking. Sweet," he says, leaning in and pressing his lips to mine once more.

This one is short. He moves back to his seat, resting his head back against the rest while I observe him intently. He closes his eyes for a few seconds before opening them just in time to watch the light turn green, telling us we can pull out of the tunnel.

He grips the wheel, and all that I can think about is those same hands gripping the back of my neck as he guided me to where he wanted me. We travel through town, and it's not until he hits the highway that he speaks.

"Tell me."

I clear my throat. "Tell you what?"

THE *Kissing* GAMES

"Ten, right?" he asks. He glances over quickly before placing his gaze back on the road.

I have a choice here. I can tell him the truth and have to live with his smugness over the next several weeks, hell, for a lifetime, because telling him that it was the best kiss of my life surely would be something he would love to remind me of every chance he got.

Or, I can tell him he's only slightly improved. I know him well enough to know that he's going to want to try again. That he's going to want to prove his skills, and just that simple thought sets a fire inside of me and has heat pooling between my thighs.

"Six." The answer is out before I can stop it, and Lord help me, I have no regrets. Not if he kisses me like that the next time. Besides, I've already decided that I'll be looking for new employment. I might as well enjoy being kissed like I'm the oxygen he needs to breathe and make the most out of having to spend time with him.

It's just a few kisses. A game of sorts. What could it hurt?

"Six?" he asks in disbelief.

I shrug as if I'm unaffected, even though I'm anything but. "You improved."

"You're fucking with me."

"Why would I lie? I'm sorry that you can't handle the truth, Spencer." I'm probably going to hell, but it's just a little white lie. No one is getting hurt unless you count his ego, and then we might have a problem.

"No fucking way, Charlie. That was—" He stops himself. "That was not a six, and you know it."

"Better luck next time," I say, teasing him.

"Is that a challenge?"

"What? No. It's just a figure of speech."

"You liked it. You're scoring me low, so I'll keep kissing you."

Damn. "Whatever," I say flippantly.

He reaches over and places his hand on my thigh. "Don't worry, baby. I think I'm going to like this game."

We're only a few miles outside of Bridgewater, and he leaves his hand on my thigh until we pull into the parking lot at the back of the building, and I don't hate it.

# Chapter
## TEN

 Spencer

Tossing the folder on my desk, I plop down in my chair. I tilt my head back and close my eyes as I let the meeting I just held float away. I've been dreading this all week, but I had to tell the board something. Last week I assured them that this was a done deal. They knew I was visiting all locations of the practice last Friday, and they expected me to tell them the contract had been signed and my plans for branding and incorporating the new asset into our current hospital system was complete.

Instead, they got me telling them that I wanted some more time. I spewed bullshit about protecting our investment and that I wanted to spend more time to get a feel for the operations and the staff that we were ensuring would keep their jobs unless something disciplinary happened. I don't need more time. The buyout is a sound business decision.

It's all a ruse. A ruse to get more time with her. Currently, I'm not her boss. We don't work for the same organization, and I feel this deep-seated need to push time so that when I'm kissing her, I don't have to worry about a sexual harassment suit. Not that Charlotte would ever do that. No, she wants my lips on hers. I can feel it every time she kisses me back.

It's not even that I'll be her boss. She will report to the Director of Physician Services, who reports to me, so she won't be a direct report. I just need an excuse to be around her. To spend time with her, even it if is under the guise that I need more intel on the operations and staff.

I'm finding that I'll do anything for just a moment with Charlotte Krause.

A knock on my door pulls me out of my thoughts. "Come in," I call out, sitting up in my chair.

"Hey, Spencer." Lucia, the hospital's director of Physician Services, smiles at me.

It took me months to get the staff to call me by my first name instead of Mr. Pennington. Everyone except for Lucia. She's been batting those eyes of hers at me, giving off fuck-me vibes from here to Texas since day one. Not once have I considered her attempt to lure me into her web.

"What can I do for you, Lucia?"

She steps further into the room and takes a seat across from my desk. "Just checking in to see what I need to do for the onboarding of the new pediatric practice that we're buying," she says.

"Nothing." I try to keep the bite of irritation out of my tone. She's just doing her job.

She furrows her brow. "I thought that the administrator was going to report to me?" There is an equal amount of hurt and anger in her tone.

"That's still the hierarchy of your positions, but there are a few final things that need to be examined before the deal is final." Like me kissing the hell out of said administrator, she's so eager to have under her.

*She's not the only one.*

"Oh. Okay. Well, is there anything I can do to help?" she asks eagerly.

THE *Kissing* GAMES

"I'll be sure to let you know if there is."

"If you need me to stay late or whatever...." Her voice trails off, and the smile on her face tells me she wants me to read between the lines.

I'm reading between those lines just fine, but that doesn't mean that I have to like what they say. Giving in to Lucia would be like drinking unsweetened tea when you have the option for sweet. There is no comparison.

"I'm all set. How are things with the new oncologist?" I ask, changing the subject and circling the conversation back to work. She rambles on about the new oncologist we hired, and I'm only half listening. It's been a week today since I've seen Charlotte, and I'm craving her like a junkie who needs his next hit.

She's always affected me. I accepted that fact years ago when we were in college that I would never be anything more to Charlotte than her rival—the guy she liked to compete and spar with. That was before I tasted her. Before I felt her smooth, soft skin under the palm of my hand, and before I felt the silky strands of her hair between my fingers.

I spent this week pretending I didn't need to see her. I've worked late every single night. So much so that even Linc commented on the hours I've been keeping. He left Monday to go back to his place that he was sharing with Audrey, who is now living with Charlotte.

"Spencer?" Lucia says, and I shake out of my thoughts and give her my attention. "Should I schedule a catch-up with Dr. Montoya?" she asks of our new oncologist.

"No. That won't be necessary." She nods and hesitates before standing.

"Call me if you need me. Anytime," she says. Her voice is lower, as if she's trying to be sexy. She's not, well, maybe she is, but she's not to me. My idea of sexy is a blue-eyed, auburn-haired long-legged beauty who's had me chasing her and my tail for the last ten years.

Lucia leaves my office, and I stare at the open door. Knowing that I can't hold off any longer, I stand, close the door, and settle back behind my desk. Grabbing my cell, I hit Charlotte's contact and place the phone next to my ear. It rings once, twice, and three times before she answers.

"Hello." I can hear the uncertainty in her voice.

"Good afternoon, Charlie."

"Spencer." She's not just saying my name. She breathes it as if hearing from me puts air into her lungs.

"Missed you this week." Those four words shock even me. That's not at all what I meant to say, but it's what I was thinking, so I'm not surprised the words passed my lips. It's too late to take them back. Not that I would if I could. I think it's time to take a different approach with my Charlie. In the past, I've always been on the defensive. I think it's time to change the play.

"It's been a week." I can hear it in her voice. She, too, has been counting the days since the last time we saw each other. That's as close as a confession that I'm going to get from her, at least for now. I'm going to wear her down.

"What does your schedule look like Monday?" I can't wait another full week to see her. I want to curse Lincoln for ending things with Audrey, taking away my random chances to see her, but then again, we might not have shared the moments that we have if that didn't happen.

"What do you need?" she asks.

"I'd like to go over the staff for each location. Attendance records, any disciplinary actions, skill sets, performance appraisals, things like that."

"For every staff member?" she asks.

"Yes. The contract states that the employment of current staff will be secured. I need to know what we are getting into and if there need to be any exceptions."

"Okay." So easily, she concedes to what I'm asking of her. We both know it's complete bullshit, but she doesn't call me out on it. I know if this were one month ago or even two weeks ago, she would have.

Progress in the making.

"We'll start with the Charleston location."

"So, you'll come here?"

THE *Kissing* GAMES

"Yeah, I'll be there. What time do you get to work?"

"Eight."

"I'll be there at eight."

"Okay. I'll start gathering everything that you need. When I started, I transitioned us to electronic for these kinds of things, so we'll have paper and electronic files. I'm only one person, and due to the confidentiality of the materials, I'm really the only person other than the physicians who have better things to do with their time that could scan items."

"Electronic is a good idea. You're a jack-of-all-trades, huh?"

"I'm everything the practice needs me to be."

In my head, I hear her telling me that she'll be anything that I need her to be, and my cock swells at the thought of her being mine. I clear my throat. "Monday, 8:00 a.m. I'll see you then," I tell her.

"I have it on my calendar. Would you like the number to my direct line at my desk so that you don't have to call my cell?"

"Do you have an issue with me calling your cell?"

She hesitates. "No," she finally replies.

I smile. I'm sure if anyone were to walk into my office right this moment, I look like I've lost my mind, grinning like a fool while on a work call. "Cell phone it is. I'll see you on Monday."

"See you Monday."

"Have a good weekend, Charlie."

"You too, Spence."

The line goes dead, but the smile on my face grows. I bet she doesn't even realize that she just called me Spence. Damn, this woman, she's taking over my mind. I don't know how I'm going to stop constantly thinking about her, but what I do know is that for the first time in my life, I'm ready for the weekend to pass quickly and for Monday to roll around.

After talking to Charlie yesterday, the rest of my day flew by. I was more productive in a few hours of the afternoon than I had been all week. Just talking to her, hearing her voice, pulled me out of my "missing Charlotte" slump I've found myself in. I know that's why. What I don't know is what I'm going to do about it. I can feel her starting to soften up to me, but I've been shot down by that woman more times than I care to admit. Sure, she thought I was joking every time I asked her out after the very first time. I might have been teasing to get under her skin, but I was still serious.

I thought that I'd let this go when we left college, but I find myself right back where I started when I laid eyes on her that very first day of freshman year. I'm consumed by her, but this time it's more. I've tasted her, and now it's more than just wanting to take a pretty girl out on a date.

I fucking crave her.

I'm sitting on the couch, scrolling through the TV, looking for something to watch, and nothing jumps out at me. I should go out and mow the lawn, but it's hot as hell outside, so I'm going to wait and do that tomorrow morning. Maybe I should call one of my buddies and see if they want to go grab some dinner. As soon as the thought crosses my mind, my cell rings. Glancing at the screen, I see "Linc calling."

"What's up?"

"I'm starving," he replies.

"You're a big boy. Make yourself something to eat." I'm still a little miffed at him over the whole waiting until the wedding weekend to break things off with Audrey.

"Have you eaten yet?"

"No." I'm not going to make this easy on him, even though it's as if he read my mind all the way from his place.

"Let's meet at High Tide for wings."

"What time?" I ask this like I have a full agenda for the rest of the day when the truth of the matter is that I have shit else to do.

"Now."

"You're buying," I tell him.

He laughs. "Fine. Let's go, grumpy. I'm withering away to nothing over here. I skipped breakfast and only had a banana for lunch."

"Why?"

THE *Kissing* GAMES

"I was caught up with going over some reports for next week and lost track of time."

"We really need to work on this workaholic thing you've got going for you."

"You know how it is," he says with a heavy sigh.

"You're right. I do know. I run a hospital, and I still manage to get away from the office. You have to let it go. You can't work yourself to the ground until you lose all sense of yourself outside of your career."

"I know. I know," he repeats. "I'm working on it." What he doesn't need to say is this is why he called off the wedding. The life he lives isn't a good life for him, let alone for Audrey, or any woman for that matter.

"If you ever plan on having a family one day, Linc, you need to get a handle on that shit."

"Trust me. I know." He pauses, and I let the silence hang between us. "High Tide in twenty. If you're not there, I'm ordering without you."

"I'll be there." It's on the tip of my tongue to tell him that if I make a commitment, I stand behind it but think better of it and keep my mouth shut. It's his life, and even if I don't agree with how he handled things, I understand why.

"Later," he mumbles, and I don't bother with a reply, knowing that he's already hung up the phone. Instead, I pull my lazy ass from the couch and head off to find my shoes.

Fifteen minutes later, I'm pulling into the parking lot of High Tide. I park next to Linc, who appears to already be inside if his empty vehicle is any indication. As soon as I walk in the door, I spot him sitting at one of the high tops talking to a waitress.

"There he is." He smiles.

"What can I get you to drink?" she asks me.

"Sweet tea for now." I look over at Linc as I slide into a chair. "Have you ordered?"

"Not yet."

"I'll give you a few minutes," the waitress says before she saunters away.

THE *Kissing* GAMES

"You're not drinking?"

I shrug. "Just not feeling it." He eyes me suspiciously but doesn't say anything. I had planned on a cold beer with my wings until I got here.

"So, how's it been being back at your place?" I ask him as the waitress places our drinks on the table.

"Are you ready to order?" she asks.

"I'll take a dozen boneless garlic parmesan wings and onion rings," Linc orders.

She turns to me.

"A dozen boneless mild and cheese sticks." I hand her the menu and turn my gaze back to my best friend, waiting for his reply.

"It's strange, man. It's lonely, and I'm not going to lie and say that I don't miss her. I do. She's been my constant, and now she's not there. I just need to adjust to my new normal without her."

I nod because what can I say to that? He loved her, but he's not in love with her. I could continue to give him shit for his decision, but at the end of the day, it was his to make.

"How's work?" he asks to change the subject.

A grin tilts my lips, and he looks at me with a question in his eyes. "Good. Working on a buyout for a local pediatric office."

"I thought that was already on lockdown?"

I nod. "Just some fine-print last-minute stuff. The deal is as good as done." I don't know why I don't tell him that it's the same practice that Charlotte works for. I guess I just want to keep her and that knowledge to myself for a little while longer. Besides, what would I tell him? That I enjoy the hell out of kissing his now ex-future sister-in-law? Nah, Lincoln has been around since the day I met her. He'll read too much into it.

"Nice— Oh, shit," he says, his shoulders falling.

"What?"

"Don't look now, but Charlotte and Audrey just walked in."

I look because, of course, I fucking do. This is Charlotte we're talking about. If she's in my orbit, I have to lay eyes on her. They're making their way to a table closer to the bar. Charlotte's long auburn hair hangs in loose waves down her back, and she's wearing a jean skirt and a tank top. Nothing spectacular. More than half of the women in this bar are dressed the same way, but none of them stand out the way Charlotte does.

"I'm going to go," Linc says as the waitress appears at our table. "Can I get a to-go box? I'm sorry," he tells her.

"Sure. I'll be right back. Do you want one too?" she asks me.

I know that I should go. I know that I should support my best friend, but the woman who has consumed my every thought for the last two weeks is here, and I'm taking that as a sign. "No, thank you."

"Sorry, man," Lincoln replies.

"It's all good. It's going to be like this for a while, but the two of you talked, right?"

"Yeah, we did. We're good. We both know this is what was best, but it's still pretty raw, and I don't want to put her through that. I'm going to slip out."

"I got the bill," I tell him as the server brings him a box.

"You sure?"

"Positive. You can get the next."

"Thanks, Spence. I'll call you later." He quickly dumps his plate into the to-go box, slides off his stool, and moves out the door as quickly as he can.

As for me, I move to his seat so that I can see the girls. I watch as they talk, and Audrey gives Charlie a hug and disappears out the door. Looks like she noticed Lincoln too. My guess is they're both leaving to avoid the other. I'm picking up my plate and my sweet tea and moving toward her table before I can think better of it.

"Looks like your company bailed too," I say when I reach her.

Charlotte glances up at me and smiles softly. "Yeah, I think it's just too soon." She doesn't need to elaborate. We both know she's referring to Lincoln and Audrey seeing each other.

"Mind if I join you?" I ask, setting my plate and drink on the counter.

"Sure."

I was going to anyway, and we both know it. This night just got a whole lot more interesting.

THE *Kissing* GAMES

# Chapter ELEVEN

*Charlotte*

I SHOULD HAVE INFORMED HIM I was leaving. I should have left with my sister, but something told me to stay. Part of me hoped that Spencer might stop and say hello. I haven't seen him this week. I thought that I would have, and I refuse to think about why I wanted to see him. I tell myself it's just what I expected. Not what I wanted.

However, here I am, telling him he can keep me company when I know it's a bad idea. I sip my beer, not really tasting it, as Spencer takes the stool next to mine.

"Are you eating?" he asks.

"I wasn't going to."

He slides his plate closer to me. "Help me out, Charlie." He nods toward his plate. "We both know the wings here are like crack and don't get me started on the ooey-gooeyness of the cheese sticks."

I can't help it. I smile. "Is that your professional opinion, Mr. CEO?" There is teasing in my tone, and it's friendly, not at all filled with the venom our barbs usually hold.

"It is if that's what it takes for you to eat with me."

I look down at the plate. The food does look delicious, and my sister and I were planning on eating. When Audrey left, I decided I was going to finish my drink and head home, but now, I might stay a little longer than planned. I'd blame the alcohol, but this is my first, and it's not even half empty.

"Let me help." I watch as Spencer picks up a cheese stick, dips it into the pizza sauce, and holds it up for me. "Open for me, Charlie."

My mouth opens without my consent, and he places the cheesy goodness in my mouth. I take a bite and pull back. I take my time chewing as I watch him take the rest of the cheese stick and pop it into his mouth.

Why is that hot? Not just him feeding me, telling me to open for him, but the fact that we're sharing a meal, and he's eating food I've already eaten from. It's intimate and not us at all. That doesn't stop me from parting my lips when he repeats the process, and I again take another delicious bite.

My eyes lock with his as I chew, and the intensity of his stare has heat pooling between my thighs. "Good girl," he says huskily.

I choke as I swallow and reach for my glass. I take a hefty drink as Spencer places his hand on the center of my back and rubs soothing circles. His touch feels like fire even through my shirt, and everyone knows you are supposed to stay away from fire, but I find myself leaning into him anyway.

"You all right?" he asks. He's close. Too close.

"I'm good." Part of me wants to take another bite, so he'll tell me what a good girl I am, but I tamp that down. This is Spencer, my rival, the guy who made our entire college careers a competition. I don't need his praise, even though those two words affected me more than I care to admit. So much so these panties are ruined.

"I need to run to the restroom." I stand on shaking legs and move through the small crowd to the ladies' room. As soon as I'm inside, I can think clearly. With my hands braced on the edge of the sink, I stare at my reflection in the mirror. My eyes are bright, my cheeks flushed, and I can still feel his hand on my back.

"He's just a man," I mutter as I step away from the sink and into the stall. I didn't need to use the bathroom, but I did need to clean up. As predicted, my panties are a mess, and there is no cleaning up. Not here. With few options, I slip off my thong, wrap it tightly in some toilet paper, and shove them into my small handbag. It's not ideal to be in this skirt without panties, but driving home in wet panties isn't ideal either.

I'm going straight home. I can't be trusted to be alone with this man right now. I need some distance to get myself together. He's going to be my boss.

My. Boss.

Squaring my shoulders, I mentally prepare myself to walk out of this bathroom and right out the door. My drink is already paid for, and I have no reason to stick around. Just because I told Spencer he could sit in the empty seat next to me doesn't mean I have to stick around to keep him company.

I'm definitely not doing that. I'm going home to get lost in a book where the hero tells the heroine she's a good girl, and I will not under any circumstance remember the sound of Spencer's voice as I read those words.

Nope. Not ever.

Exhaling a deep breath, I pull open the door only to be greeted with warm chocolate eyes. "Spencer." I breathe his name.

"You were gone a while," he says. He's standing casually against the opposite wall with his hands shoved deep in his pockets and one leg bent, resting on the wall.

"There was a line." It's a lie, and we both know it, but he doesn't call me out on it.

I stand frozen as his eyes roam over every inch of me. I should walk away, but my feet won't move. Instead, I stand as still as a statue while he looks his fill. My mind immediately goes to my ruined thong that's shoved into my purse.

Spencer stands to his full height and takes one step, then stops. I'm still blocking the door. It's just us in the dimly lit area. "It's been seven days since I've laid eyes on you," he tells me.

"Are you keeping a diary now?" The bite that should have been in my tone isn't there. Instead, it's nothing but curiosity which I know he hears.

"What makes you think I just started it?" he asks. He takes another step toward me, a small one, still leaving space between us.

"You expect me to believe that all these years, you've been keeping track of the last time you saw me?" I tilt my head to the side to study him. I can't seem to get a good read on his motives. Why would he want me to think that?

"No diary, Charlie girl," he says softly.

"Excuse me," a woman who looks to have had about five too many beers says as she stumbles toward me.

Spencer reaches out and snakes an arm around my waist, and pulls me into his chest as we step out of the way. We're now further down the darkened hallway. There's practically no light, and I know that no one will see us unless they're actually searching. There's no one here tonight that will be looking for me, or for him for that matter. We're all alone. You would think that I'd be scared, and that's the reason my heart is racing, but that's not it. It's him. Being this close to him. The feel of his large hand gripping my hip, the way my hands rest on his strong muscular chest, and the way he dips his head, burying his face in my neck and breathing me in.

"You smell so good. Like sunshine and... you."

"Me?"

"Yeah, I don't know what it is, but I only smell it when I'm close to you." He pulls me closer, to where my arms are now trapped between us. I should step away. I should try to break out of his hold, but I remain motionless.

"Dance with me, Charlie," he says, wrapping his arms around me and holding me close.

"Here?"

"Yeah, right here."

"We should move to the dance floor." There's zero intent behind my words. They're empty, and his deep chuckle tells me that he knows it.

"Why would we do that when I can have you all to myself?" He runs his hand up and down my spine, and my body melts into him without further prompting. Am I so starved for a man's affection that I'll give in to my rival?

No. I'm not, and he's not really my rival, not anymore. After the last few weeks, I'm not certain he ever was. Was it all in my head? The competition, the barbs back and forth? What was it if not rivalry? Some kind of twisted foreplay? Besides, I know without a shadow of a doubt I wouldn't be this turned on by just any man. For some reason, it's only Spencer who makes me feel this way.

I want to ask him why he wants me all to himself, but to be honest, I'm afraid of the answer. Lines are being blurred, and my body's reaction to him is confusing. I shouldn't want Spencer Pennington to wrap me in his arms and never let go. He's not the man for me, even for one night. He's my future boss, my college rival, and the best friend of the man who broke my sister's heart.

I shouldn't want him.

That doesn't stop me from pushing my arms from between us and wrapping them around his waist. That doesn't stop me from resting my head on his chest. He barely sways in the dark corner of this hallway to some country tune blaring over the bar speakers. It doesn't stop me from thinking about how it would feel to have one night with him.

Just one.

"Just one what?" he asks, his voice soft.

*Shit.* "Nothing," I murmur without lifting my head, praying like hell he'll let it go.

"Just one what, Charlie girl?" he asks again.

"D-Dance. Just one dance."

He leans back just enough so that I lift my head, and he turns us so that my back is pressed against the wall. "You're lying," he says matter-of-factly. "You hesitated, and the Charlie I know never hesitates. Tell me what you want, Charlotte, and I'll give it to you."

"It's nothing."

I gasp when he leans in and presses his lips to my neck, just beneath my ear. "It's not nothing if it's on your mind. Tell me. I can't make it happen if I don't know what it is."

"What makes you think you can make it happen?" I ask, and he smirks, which causes me to curse under my breath. I just gave myself away.

"We're already dancing, Charlie girl." His lips move to my ear. His hot breath causes shivers to race down my spine. He pulls me closer. His body is now molded to mine, and I'm pressed up against the wall. We're completely hidden from sight.

"Fine. You're so full of yourself. I was wondering what it would be like to be with you for one night." I start to explain further, but I know I'm digging myself into a hole here, so I need to keep my mouth shut.

"Let's find out." Before I know what's happening, his lips are on mine. His kiss is like a storm, a tornado that rips through everything I thought I knew. Rips through everything I thought I wanted.

I kiss him back.

This isn't the first time his lips have been on mine, but it is the first time his large hands have roamed my body. One hand slides from my hip over my thigh, and then he reaches bare skin just beyond my skirt. He growls and pulls my leg up to wrap around him.

Oh, God. I'm bare, and all it would take was one small move for him to notice. I should stop this. I should push him away, but he deepens this kiss, his tongue gliding with mine as if we've done this very thing every day for the last ten years.

His hand moves up my bare thigh beneath my skirt, and when he reaches my hip, he freezes. He pulls away from our kiss to rest his forehead against mine. "Charlie, baby, are you bare right now? Are you walking around in this sexy-ass skirt with no panties?" he asks, his voice is thick and gravelly.

His hard cock is pressing against my belly, and that's my only excuse for the words that come out of my mouth next. "You ruined my panties," I blurt.

"Start talking, Charlotte." He's using what I imagine is his CEO voice when he wants things to go his way.

"What do you want me to say?"

"Where are your panties?"

THE *Kissing* GAMES

"In my purse. Wrapped in toilet paper," I add, because apparently, once I start talking, I can't stop.

His hand moves to rest just above my pussy that's aching for his touch. "Tell me what you liked. What did I do? What did I say? Tell me so that I can do it again. And again, and again. Tell me, Charlie," he pleads.

"This is embarrassing. Can we just let this go?"

He laughs. Not just a chuckle, but a full "body shaking, head tossed back" laugh. "If you think for one second that you're going to stand here looking sexy as fuck and tell me that you had to take your panties off because I made your pussy so wet they were drenched and that I'm just going to let that go, you're wrong. So very, very wrong, Charlie." He leans in close, his thumb tracing just above where I need it to be beneath my skirt, and presses a feather-soft kiss to my lips. "Tell me."

"Fine." I roll my eyes and mentally remind myself that I've already decided to look for another job. I'll never be able to face him after this. I mean, I'll have to for a while, but not forever. No way. "You were feeding me, which is intimate, and then you called me a good girl."

"Put your arms around my neck."

"What?" I ask, confused.

"Put your arms around my neck, Charlie. I'm going to lift you, and I want your legs wrapped around me."

"Someone might see," I protest, but it's weak at best.

"Never." His voice is full of conviction. "I'll never let anyone see you like that. They'll see your bare legs and my back, and that's only if they come looking for us in the shadows. Arms around my neck."

What the hell, right? I mean, I'm already in this deep. What are another few minutes of this man's hands and lips on me? Something tells me it's a memory I'll never forget. So, I go against all better judgment and place my hands around his neck.

His palms move to the back of my bare thighs, but not before each grabs a handful of ass, giving it a gentle yet firm squeeze. "Legs around my waist," he says gruffly.

Doing as I'm told, I lock my ankles once my legs are wrapped tightly around him. "Good girl," he murmurs. My body quakes, and I can feel him grin as he presses a tender kiss to my collarbone.

I open my mouth to scold him, but the combination of his hard cock resting just where I need him to be, with only his jeans separating us and his lips nipping and sucking at my neck, I can't seem to find my voice.

"Tell me I can touch you, Charlie. Tell me that I can take care of that ache between your thighs. Let me show you what a night for us would look like."

I part my lips to tell him no. This is crazy. We can't do this. "Okay," I whisper instead, and I'm not mad about it. Not at all. Especially not when one hand slips between us and his thumb finally finds my clit.

"Oh," I moan, resting my head back against the wall.

He keeps his thumb drawing lazy circles on my clit, which is doing delicious things to my body, and manages to take another finger and trace it through my desire for him. "Is all this for me?" he rasps. "I need to hear you say it, Charlie. Is this for me? Is your pussy crying for me?" he grates.

"Y-Yes."

"Good girl."

"Fuck," I mumble as a fresh wave of desire washes over me. He's going to have a huge-ass wet spot on his jeans.

He chuckles. "I don't give a fuck about my jeans, Charlie girl. All I care about is you and giving you what you need. Do you need to come?"

"Please."

"I wish we weren't here," he says gruffly. I stiffen, and he's quick to explain. "Not here in this darkened hallway of High Tide. I wish we were at my place, in my bed, where I could see you. Where I could taste you. You're not getting the full experience here, sweetheart."

"I'm good with half." He rocks his hard cock into my core. "Half is so good," I tell him.

"Promise me you'll give me another shot at this. You'll let me take you on my bed or fuck me, your bed, and you'll let me worship you. Tell me I get another chance."

"Depends on your rating, and right now, you're at a zero, Pennington," I say, trying to rile him up so that he'll give me what I want.

"Is this an extension of our kissing game?" he asks, humor evident in his tone.

"It's whatever it needs to be for you to make me come. Please, Spencer."

"This is how this is going to go. We're not rating tonight unless it's our kisses. I'll give you what you need, but I need a redo. Immediately. I need to show you what it's like to truly be cherished, and I can't do that here."

"Fine. Yes. Okay. Whatever."

"Promise me, Charlotte."

"I promise. Just get on with it already before someone catches us."

"My pleasure," he says. The next thing I know, his thumb presses harder than before while he thrusts his hips, and his lips capture mine. It feels as though he has ten hands, and they're everywhere as I draw closer to the abyss of pleasure he's offering.

"Spenc—" I can't even form his full name as his thrusts grow faster. I rock my hips, and that's all it takes. I fly high and feel as though I'm falling at the same time, but in reality, my back is still braced against the wall, and Spencer's hold on me is firm. My orgasm rolls through my body like a tsunami. Wave after wave of pleasure, unlike anything I've ever felt before. When I finally feel human again, I open my eyes to find his dark chocolate eyes watching me intently.

"That was the sexiest thing I've ever seen in my life." He kisses me hard before helping me stand back on my feet. He makes sure my skirt is pulled down and that I'm steady before releasing me.

"I... should be getting home."

He nods. "Come on, baby. I'll walk you out." He slides his arm around my waist and pulls me into his side, and I lean into him. He walks me to my car and opens the door for me. "Are you sure you're good to drive?" he asks.

"I'm sure."

"You have two choices. You call me when you get home, or I can follow you home."

"I'm an adult, Spencer. I'm capable of getting myself home safely."

"Two choices." He holds up two fingers.

"I'll call you when I get home," I grumble.

"Good girl." He smirks as he leans in and presses a soft kiss to my lips. "Drive safe." He steps back and waits for me to buckle my seat belt before closing the door and rapping his knuckles on the hood of my car.

I give him what I hope is a bright smile. This is never happening again. The drive home is only ten minutes, and my mind races the entire drive. When I pull into the driveway, I'm grateful the house is dark. There's no way to hide that something is up, especially from my sister.

Once in the house, I strip down and turn on the shower before texting Spencer.

> **Me:**      Made it home safe.

My phone rings, and I see his name. "Hello?"

"You were supposed to call."

"I texted you instead."

"I needed to hear that you were safe, Charlie. Anyone could have had your phone."

"And this random person knew that I was supposed to text you?" I laugh.

"Next time, call me like you're supposed to."

"There won't be a next time," I tell him.

"You made me a promise tonight, Charlie."

"We'll see." I'll avoid him, and he'll forget all about the promise I made in the heat of the moment.

"Yeah," he agrees. "We'll see." He doesn't sound convinced, but that's okay. He'll get the hint eventually.

"Sweet dreams, Charlie girl."

My heart softens to him. "Night, Spence."

# Chapter TWELVE

Spencer

TOSSING MY PHONE ONTO THE bed, I strip out of my clothes and move to the bathroom. Turning on the shower, I don't wait for the water to warm before I step under the spray. The ice-cold liquid hits my skin and feels like needles. I stand still and take the abuse. My cock hangs heavy between my thighs, and the ache has been constant since laying eyes on her earlier tonight.

The cold water does nothing for my situation. I froze my ass off for no reason. The only thing that will help is release or Charlotte, and I don't see option two happening tonight or anytime soon. I'm going to have to settle for my hand and some self-love. This won't be the first time that I've jerked off to the image of the auburn-haired goddess, and I'm certain it won't be the last.

Taking hold of my cock, I squeeze as I close my eyes. I grip the base as my hand glides to the top and back again. An image of her sky-blue eyes filled with desire as she peered up at me earlier tonight is all I can see. And what do I hear? It's her moans as her orgasm soared through her body.

I did that.

I gave her that pleasure.

*Fuck.* My grip grows tighter. My strokes faster. Those blue eyes are all I see as I chase my release. Tingles shoot up my spine as my body grows taut. With one hand braced on the shower wall, I hang my head and move my hand faster and faster, chasing the high. With two more long, fast strokes, I'm spilling everything I wanted to give her tonight down the drain. My cock twitches in my palm as my chest heaves with exertion. Just the thought of her was all it took to have me falling over the edge of pleasure.

I wish it wasn't just the memory of her and that she was here with me right now. This isn't a new wish, but somehow, it's different. I feel like I'm actually getting to know the real Charlotte.

I let the hot water rain down on me while I catch my breath. I think about the last few weeks and my interactions with Charlotte. She's not the stuck-up woman with the attitude that says I'm better than you that I thought that she was. The only thing I was right about when it comes to Charlotte is that she is the most beautiful woman I've ever laid eyes on.

Tonight, the way she responded to my touch…. I'm still shocked she let me touch her at all, but my guess is that she didn't realize what she was doing. She didn't know that I was now addicted. She didn't know that she'd awakened the beast inside me, the one that wants her. Only her. If I thought her kisses were potent, I had no idea what it would feel like to have her in my arms, my fingers inside her, and my name on her lips as she lost control.

I want her.

I've always wanted her.

I know that I need to tread lightly. I know Charlotte well enough to understand that she's going to try to push what happened between us under the rug. She's going to pretend that it never happened, and although I'll never forget tonight, I need to not push her. Not too far. I need to move us forward without being obvious about it. I have no fucking clue how I'm going to make that happen, but I'm going to give it all that I've got. Because at the end of the day, the fact remains the same. I want Charlotte Krause to be mine.

It's Monday morning, and I barely slept last night. A hundred different scenarios of how today was going to go ran through my mind. I still don't know what to expect. I have narrowed it down to one of two things. She's either going to pretend it never happened or tell me that it was a mistake and will never happen again.

I'm not okay with either.

It did happen, and I'm going to fight like hell for it to happen again. Something tells me that this battle is going to be the hardest I've faced, but in the end, the victory will be sweet. I refuse to accept anything less. We've danced around this for ten years. I've misjudged her, and it's time we get back on the right track. The one that should have started that first day freshman year when she turned me down. I let my ego get in the way, blaming it on hers when I should have fought for what I wanted. I was young, but now I'm older and wiser, and I'm damn certain that she is who I want.

It's twenty minutes until eight, and her car is already here. I wonder if she had trouble sleeping last night as well. I reached for my phone more times than I care to admit to call or text her, but I stopped myself every single time. I don't care that I'm early. I'm eager to see her. Grabbing my bag that holds my laptop and the contract, which I pretty much have memorized by this point, I climb out of my car and make my way inside.

"Good morning. How may I help you?" the receptionist greets me.

"I have an appointment with Charlotte," I tell her.

"You must be Mr. Pennington. She told me she was expecting you. I'll take you back to the conference room." She pushes the security button that releases the door, and I walk through, waiting for her to guide me down the hall to the conference room. I don't bother telling her that I know my way around or that I'm about to be her boss's boss's boss. "Here we are." She smiles kindly. "I'll let Charlotte know that you're here."

"Thank you, Anne," I say, reading her name tag. She blushes and scurries off down the hallway. Instead of taking a seat in one of the many chairs, with my bag still slung over my shoulder, I move to the window and peer outside. It's a nice warm day, the sun is shining, and I have a feeling it's going to be a good one. It has to be. I get to spend the day with her.

"Good morning," her sweet voice says from behind me.

I take my time turning to face her. "Morning, Charlie girl," I say softly. I watch as her eyes flash with recognition, and her cheeks pinken just barely, but the color is there as she remembers the last time I called her that.

Her shoulders fall, and she closes her eyes, pulling in a calming breath. "Spencer," she whispers.

"Shall we get started?" I interrupt her. I know that she's going to tell me it was a mistake, and I don't want to hear that. It wasn't a mistake.

"Sure. I have the files here for the non-clinical staff. I thought we could work our way through the staff list that way."

"That works for me. This should be an easy process. I really just want to know if there are any problem employees and get an idea of educational background."

"Okay." She nods as she sets the files on the table and takes a seat.

I walk around the table and take the seat next to hers. There's still too much space between us, but I'll have to make do for now.

"How do you want to do this?" she asks, turning to look at me.

"Let's just start with the first file on the stack."

"Okay. Well, first, we have Anne Anderson. Anne is a receptionist who works full time. She's been here for six years. She's a great employee and has never had any type of disciplinary action. She's pleasant, and the parents and kids love her. She just has one of those personalities that she can charm anyone," she says with a soft chuckle.

"The Anne that's at the front desk today?" I ask.

"That would be her."

I nod. "Good. Next."

"Next, we have Brenda. She works in medical records. She's been here for twenty-three years and only works three days a week. Two, if the workload is low. She takes care of all medical records requests for transfers in and out of the practice. No disciplinary action, and she's a delight."

"Good. We have a medical records department that she can work closely with."

"Is her job safe? She truly is an asset to the practice."

"Charlie, we don't plan on cutting any jobs. From what I've seen and the financial reports tell me, it's true all three locations run like well-oiled machines. This is just me doing my homework." Homework that's unnecessary, but it gives me time with her. Time with the Charlotte that's not competing with me and throwing insults my way. Then again, I've not been on my best behavior either. I'm not innocent in the rivalry of our past.

"Thank you. I know we've talked about this, and Dr. Phillips assured me as well, but the staff at all three locations are good people. Most of them live paycheck to paycheck, and I worry for them."

"Not for you?"

"For me too, but I know that I have my MBA to fall back on. I might have to drive out of Charleston, but I have more options than they do."

"They respect you."

"How do you know?"

"It's obvious. There is no boss in the history of bosses that cares this much and doesn't have the respect of the staff."

She nods. "They're family to me," she says softly. "As you know, Audrey and I lost our parents when we were young. It was just before I started college. Aunt Miranda is the only family we have left. Even if we did have others, you spend more time with your work family than you do your real family, and I feel as though it's important for them to feel appreciated and respected for what they do."

Her words resonate with me. "You're incredible," I tell her. I also let the truth sink in. I knew they'd lost their parents, but I didn't know when. "I'm sorry for your loss," I tell her when I realize she dropped a pretty heavy truth bomb, gave me an insight into her life she's never given me.

She nods. "Thank you. It was a long time ago, but I still miss them every day."

"So, it was right before you started college?"

"Yeah. I didn't want to go. I mean, I did, but I hated the thought of leaving Audrey behind with Aunt Miranda. It wasn't that she was neglectful, but she just wasn't the loving adult we were used to. The first few months were really hard for both of us, but we made it through it."

I think back to the first time I met her. It was freshman orientation, and while she was easily the most beautiful woman in attendance that day, she was quiet. Reserved. I chalked it up to first-day jitters and took a shot at asking her out anyway. She shut me down immediately and then again the next time, and I judged her for it. I pegged her as thinking that she was better than me, when in reality, she was grieving and missing her little sister.

"I didn't know," I say, my voice hoarse at what a fuckup I was back then. "That first day we met. I didn't know."

"Didn't know what?"

"Charlie, baby, I fucked up."

She turns her chair to face me. I do the same, and our knees are touching, but I have her full, undivided attention. "I thought you were being rude. I thought that you were blowing me off. I was intimidated by your beauty, and when you shot me down, I just assumed you thought that you were better than me. That's why I gave you such a hard time all these years."

"What?" she whispers.

Leaning forward, I rest my palm against her cheek. "I never wanted to compete with you. I never wanted to fight with you. My ego was bruised, and I made assumptions. You were grieving the loss of your parents and missing Audrey, and I treated you terribly."

"You didn't. We competed. We tossed some insults back and forth, but you were never mean to me."

"I was an asshole."

Her eyes well with tears. "I missed them. I didn't mean to be rude. I just didn't have it in me to start a new friendship or relationship. I worked my ass off for my grades to keep my scholarship. We had to sell the house to pay it off, as well as some other debt. My scholarship was my only option for staying in school. If I'd let my grades slip and lost my scholarship, I wouldn't have been able to finish. I didn't have a back-up plan."

I need to be closer to her. I need— Fuck, I don't know what I need.

I move my chair closer, her legs now between mine. I lean in close so that I hope she can see the sincerity in my eyes. "I'm so sorry. I was young, and I didn't stop to think about the fact that it could be something more, something other than you thinking you're too good for me that you turned me down. Fuck. No wonder you want nothing to do with me."

"That's not true, Spencer. I thought you hated me. You were nice that first day and even the second time we ran into each other. That time was a blur, but I remember that. Then you weren't. I immediately went on the defensive. I was competing with you as much as myself to make sure my scholarship stayed intact. I didn't care if I was top of the class. I just wanted to be in class."

Leaning in, I press my lips to her forehead. I want to do more than that. I want to pull her into my arms and hold her. I want to tell her over and over and over again how sorry I am.

It just goes to show that when you make assumptions, you truly do make an ass out of yourself. To think of all the years we wasted. If I had just kept trying, maybe she would have opened up to me like she has today. She could have been mine all this time.

"Can we start over?" I ask, my lips barely a breath from hers. I'm aware that anyone could walk into this conference room at any time and see us like this, but damn if I care. I vow in this moment to treat her like the queen that she is. I don't recall a time I was truly mean to her, but I wasn't loving her either. I could have been loving her.

I want to be loving her.

"We don't need to start over."

"Yes, we do." Sitting back in my chair, I hold out my hand. "Hi, I'm Spencer Pennington. CEO of Charleston Memorial."

She smiles, her eyes shimmering with unshed tears. "Nice to meet you, Spencer. I'm Charlotte Krause, practice administrator of this fine establishment."

"I'm very aware that I'm going to be your boss once this deal goes through. I'm also very aware of the hospital handbook. There are no rules about employees dating. You won't be reporting directly to me."

She laughs. It's a happy sound that fills the room and the crack in my heart when I learned the truth about that day. "Aren't you jumping ahead of yourself?" she asks.

"Charlie girl, I knew the minute I laid eyes on you that I wanted you to be mine. I might have been too young and too intimidated by your beauty back then, but that's not me now. I want you." I peer into her deep blue eyes, willing her to see the truth in my words.

"This is crazy, Spencer."

"Have dinner with me."

"What?"

"Have dinner with me."

"I don't think that's a good idea."

"You have to eat, right?"

"It's too early to be thinking about dinner."

"Not if I know it's going to be shared with you."

"I can't. Audrey and I are ordering in and watching a movie tonight." She pushes her chair back, putting distance between us.

"Tomorrow night? The next night? The night after that? You tell me when. I'll be there."

"I don't know this side of you."

"You're going to." There's confidence in my words.

"We should keep going." She places Brenda's file on top of Anne's and grabs the next one.

"Charlie." I wait for her to look at me. "Saturday night happened. It was hot as fuck, and we"—I point to her and then back to me—"are going to happen. You need time to let that settle in that beautiful mind of yours. I can agree to that, but I'm the type of man who learns from his mistakes, and I won't make the same one twice."

She opens her mouth to speak as a knock sounds at the door, and Dr. Phillips enters the conference room with a wide smile on his face. We make small talk, and I bullshit my way through looking at the staff files. He invites me to lunch, and although I want to decline and steal Charlotte away, I know I can't. As I agree, I see her shoulders relax out of the corner of my eye.

She thinks I'll let this go.

She's wrong.

Charlotte Krause is going to be spending a lot more time kissing this rival.

# Chapter
## THIRTEEN

*Charlotte*

THIS WEEK HAS BEEN THE longest week in history. I haven't seen Spencer since Monday. We spent the entire day going over staffing for the Charleston office, and he took every chance he had to touch me. From his hand on my arm, the small of my back, and brushing my hair out of my eyes. He's not acting like the Spencer I've come to know, and that worries me.

Not because I'm afraid of him, but because I know if he keeps this up, I won't be able to resist him. It will be a week tomorrow since our tryst at High Tide, and I can still feel his hands on me. In fact, it's pretty much all I've been thinking about.

Well, I've also been thinking about the talk we had on Monday. I had no idea he thought the things that he did. I was so closed off to my grief that I didn't even notice until it was too late, and our relationship had been formed. I've never hated him. He always annoyed me with the way he thought he was so damn charming and constantly tossed his grades in my face. I never stopped to think that there might be another reason.

I never thought I would admit this, but Spencer Pennington is a nice guy. He's also the sexiest man I've ever laid eyes on. Those two are bad enough, add in his tenacity and the sincerity in his eyes, and I'm a roller coaster of emotions.

He called me earlier asking me to go to dinner, and I told him that I had plans with my sister. It's not a lie. Audrey and I planned to stay in and watch movies all night. Then she got a call from Amara asking her to grab dinner. They invited me, but I insisted on staying home. I need some time for myself to think about this week. I also want to start looking for jobs but don't want Audrey to find out. Not until I know for sure that I've found something. I don't want her to worry. Not only that, I haven't told her yet that Spencer is going to be my new boss. I don't know why I've kept that information to myself, but I have. I planned on telling her tonight, but thanks to Amara, I have a little more time.

I know I'm the only one making a big deal out of this. Even now, when I know he's not the guy I thought he was, I still can't let him be my boss. Not when a simple look from him sets my body on fire. Not when his kisses are the best I've ever had, despite what I tell him his rating is. He knows I'm lying, and I know I'm lying. It's a game we're playing, and I can't play that game with my boss.

That brings me to my exciting Friday night. I'm curled up on the couch. My hair is in a messy knot on the top of my head, my face is wiped clean of all makeup. I'm in a pair of sleep shorts and a tank, sans bra because those things are torture devices, and my laptop is on my lap as I scroll through job postings.

When my phone rings, I assume it's my sister or my best friend, Cala. They're really the only two to ever call me unless it's one of my employees calling in sick, which is why I don't look at the screen. "Hello."

"You lied to me."

Spencer's deep voice fills my ears. He doesn't sound mad, irritated, maybe? "What are you talking about? How did I lie to you?"

"You said you were having a night in with your sister."

"That was the plan. Plans change."

"That means we can grab dinner."

"Sorry, I already ate," I say, looking at the empty pint of mint chocolate chip ice cream I devoured once I learned that Audrey was going out to dinner with Amara.

"Ice cream doesn't count, Charlie," he grumbles as there's a knock at the door.

Who in the hell could that be? "How did you know I had ice cream?" I ask as I climb off the couch and head to the front door. It's probably one of the neighborhood kids selling something for school. They all know I'm a sucker and can't say no to them.

"I ran into your sister and Amara," he says.

I pull open the door. "Like I said, plans—" I freeze when I see that Spencer is standing on my front porch. "What are you doing here?" I ask, still holding and talking into the phone.

He pulls his from his ear, taps the screen, and shoves it into his jeans pocket with one hand while the other holds up a bag from my favorite Chinese restaurant. The smell has my mouth watering, or maybe it's him. Either way, I'm starving for both, but one isn't on my meal plan.

"I brought dinner." He nods toward the bag in his hand.

"I already ate."

"Charlie, dessert is not dinner." He steps into the house, his tight muscled body pressing against my braless breasts as he enters.

*Shit. I need to put on a bra.*

"How did you know where I lived?" I ask him.

"Charleston is a small town, and your sister was all too accommodating when I told her I asked you out to dinner, but you declined because you were supposed to be having dinner with her."

"Amara called. They invited me, but I stayed home." His eyes turn toward my laptop, and I rush to close it, my bare tits swinging loose behind my tank top like two pendulums.

When I glance up at Spencer to see if he noticed, his heated gaze is staring at my chest. "I should— I need to run to my room real fast." My face is burning with embarrassment.

Before I can make a move, Spencer is in front of me, sliding an arm around my waist. "Stay. This is your home, Charlie. I'll behave."

"Do you know how to behave?" I ask.

He smirks. "I'll try to behave." He leans down and kisses my cheek. "Now sit, and I'll make us a plate. What have you got to drink?" he asks as he releases me and turns toward my kitchen. My house is an open concept, so you can see the kitchen, living room, and dining room from all angles.

Spencer starts opening cabinets until he finds plates and begins dishing up large helpings. My feet move on their own accord as I make my way to the kitchen and grab two beers out of the fridge. "This okay?" I ask, holding one of the bottles up for him to see.

"Girl after my own heart." He grins and nods.

I watch him in his white fitted T-shirt and faded jeans. His tattoos are on display, and they're sexy. *He's* sexy. I've been lying to myself all week. I can't resist him. I don't want to resist him.

"I can't eat all that," I tell him when he grabs both plates from the counter.

He shrugs. "You can try. Where are we eating? Dining room table or couch?"

"Couch."

He smiles and nods. "Looks like you had a nice little setup going."

"I was settled in for the night, just answering some emails and surfing the internet."

"Find anything interesting?"

*Oh, you know, just a few jobs that I've applied for because I'm stubborn and don't want you to be my boss.* That's not the only reason. Spencer and I have the same degree. I'd like to advance my career. It's something I knew I always wanted to do, and the buyout has given me the push I need to start my search.

"Nope." It's just a small white lie.

"You should have called me."

"Why would I do that?" I ask before taking a bite of my chicken.

"Your plans changed. You had other offers." He gives me a pointed look.

"I was perfectly content sitting my ass on this couch. I had my ice cream, and after a little web surfing, I planned to read a book."

"An entire book?"

"Yep."

"What are you reading?"

"You wouldn't like it." I can't imagine him reading about a sexy Viking.

"What? Do you think I don't read? I graduated from Clemson, too, and as I recall, our grades were pretty damn close."

"Are we going back to that?"

"We're not. I was just making a point. I read for pleasure too."

"Not this kind of pleasure," I mutter.

"What was that?"

I shake my head. I'm not telling him. Nope. No way. We are not having this conversation.

"Come on, Charlie girl. What did you say?"

I roll my eyes, and I know he's not going to let this go. "Not that kind of pleasure, but it is just a little something else too."

"Explain that."

"Romance, Spencer. I read romance."

"And they give you pleasure?"

"They do."

He points his index finger at me. "What's causing that pink hue to cover your cheeks?"

"Nothing."

"Let me read one of them."

"What?"

"I want to read one of your books. Which is your favorite? I'll read it. I'll let you know if it turns me on like it does you."

"We are not doing that."

"We are." He spies my Kindle on the table and snags it before I have a chance to stop him. He turns it on easily, and my mind flashes to the scene I was in the middle of when I stopped reading last night.

His eyes are glued to the small device. I can see him turn a few pages, and then he powers off the device and places it back on the table. He picks up the plate that he had placed on the cushion between us and continues to eat. He doesn't say a single word, and I can't read his facial expression.

"Well?" I finally ask because the suspense is killing me. Is he disgusted? Turned on? I need him to tell me.

"Eat your dinner, Charlie."

"You can't do that. You can't read my book and go back to eating like nothing happened. You're leaving this conversation open," I complain. I'm grasping at straws. I went from not wanting to have this conversation to needing him to tell me what he thinks. Suddenly, that's all that matters, because knowing what he was reading has me turned on.

"You eat. Then we'll talk about your book." His voice is deep and husky, and if I'm not mistaken, riddled with the need that I'm currently feeling.

My panties are soaked.

My palms are damp with sweat.

"Spencer."

"Eat, Charlie. I promise you we will talk about what I just read. However, I won't do it until you've been fed. Ice cream is not dinner. I'm a man of my word."

He is. Through all the years I've known him, he's always been honest. Most times, brutally so. I have no argument. He's going to give me what I want. So, I pick up my fork and continue to eat. My heart beats a little faster in my chest at his concern for me.

We both dive into our meals, not speaking. You would think that it would be awkward, but it's not. Not at all. I hate that I'm even going to admit this, even if it's only to myself, but I like him here in my home. In my wildest dreams, I never imagined we'd be here, but I can admit that I'm glad that we are.

"Thank you for dinner, Spencer," I say once I've swallowed my last bite. "I'm stuffed." I stand to take my plate to the kitchen, but his hand on my wrist stops me.

"Put the plate down, Charlotte."

I tilt my head to the side to study him. "I'm just going to put it in the dishwasher and clean up. I'll be right back."

"Leave it. I'll get it later."

"You brought dinner. I'll clean up." I try to pull my hand free, but his grip is strong.

"Charlie, baby, put the plate down." Following his own advice, he leans over and places his on the coffee table and stands from the couch, taking mine from my hands and placing it on top of his.

He laces his fingers through mine and begins to lead me out of the room down the hall. "Which room is yours?"

"My bedroom? Why do we need to go to my bedroom? What are you doing?" I rattle off a host of questions as my mind tries to register what's going on.

He stops and turns to look at me. He moves us so that my back is against the wall. He braces his hands next to my head and bends low so that I can feel his hot breath against my skin.

"We're going to your bedroom, Charlie. That book...." He nips at my ear, and my hands rest against his chest, where I grip the material of his shirt as if it's my lifeline and final connection to him.

"What about my book?" I ask as my desire flares to life. If I thought I was turned on sitting on the couch across from him, I'm now an inferno of desire.

"Do you touch yourself when you read, Charlie?"

I open my mouth to deny the truth, but the truth falls from my lips before I can. "Yes." My reply is breathless, which is exactly how he makes me feel.

"Do you think about the guy in the book?"

"Sometimes." Having him this close to me is like a truth serum. Not that I have anything to hide. I don't. Sex is natural, it's normal, and that's how we all got here.

"Who else do you think about, Charlie?" His voice is the deepest I've ever heard it.

"W-What?"

"Never mind. I don't want you to answer that," he all but growls. He drops his lips to my neck, and my body sags against the wall.

"What are we doing, Spencer?" I ask as he kisses his way up to my ear.

"What we're doing is turning your fiction into real life. No one gets to see you come undone but me." His hot breath against my ear sends shivers down my spine. Then again, maybe it's his words.

"Am I going to come undone?" I ask him.

"As soon as you tell me which room is yours."

I swallow hard as I let my mind catch up to what he's saying. He's going to turn my fiction into real life. I try really hard to think about the scene he read, but the only thing I can process right now is the feel of his body pressed against mine and the promise of falling apart for him.

"Tell me this is okay, Charlie girl. Tell me you want this as much as I do."

"Want what?" I ask breathlessly. I know what he's asking, but I need to hear him say it. To spell it out for me in black and white.

"That you want me as much as I want you. That tonight, you're going to let me make that scene in your book come alive. Do you want that, baby? Do you want me to give that to you?"

*Yes. Yes. Yes.* "This isn't us," I try to reason with my mind and with him. This isn't us, at least the college us. It appears the *us* that is post my sister's failed wedding is exactly this.

"Use that pretty mouth of yours, Charlie."

"Yes." The word slips out, but I don't regret it. I trust him. Even with our past, I know he'd never hurt me, and he's offering to take care of this ache. My pussy is drenched for him, and after last weekend, I'm ready for more.

More of him. More of whatever he's willing to give me.

"This one." I point to the door we're standing next to in the hallway. "This is my room."

"Good girl," he rasps. He kisses me hard but pulls away and takes a step back. "Go to your room. I'm going to lock up."

I part my lips to argue with him but think better of it. Instead, I nod and, on shaking legs, push open my bedroom door and move through the darkness of the room to my bed. I turn on the small lamp on my nightstand that gives the room a soft, romantic glow. My hands are clasped tightly in my lap as I anticipate what's to come.

However this night turns out, I'm already certain I'll have no regrets.

# Chapter FOURTEEN

*Spencer*

I RUSH BACK TO THE living room and make sure the door is locked before making my way to the kitchen. I check the sliding glass door and turn the light on over the stove so Audrey's not coming home to a dark house, then kill the lights, and make my way blindly back to her room. Once at her doorway, I stop and take in the scene before me.

Charlotte is sitting on her bed. The soft glow of the bedside lamp illuminates her features. Her dark auburn hair falls loosely over her shoulders, and I smile. She took her hair down for me. I'm wasting time out here when I could be devouring the beauty before me. When I step into the room, her eyes lift to mine.

"Audrey... if she comes home, she's going to see your car in the driveway."

Reaching behind my neck, I remove my T-shirt, tossing it to the floor. "Does that bother you? That she's going to know that I'm here. That I'm here with you?"

THE *Kissing* GAMES

She parts her lips to speak, but no words come out. Clear blue eyes regard me thoughtfully. "Do you care?" she asks.

I smile. I know what she's doing. She's not willing to put herself out there for us. Not yet, and that's okay. I'm willing to do it for both of us. I want her. I've always wanted her, and now it's time that I fight. For her. For us.

"I don't care that she knows that I'm here." I keep going before she can ask more questions. I know what's on her mind. "I don't care if she knows that I'm in here with you. I don't care if she knows that I want you."

"You want me?"

"I'm here for you. Not because I wanted the night to end like this, but because I wanted to see you. Spend time with you. If that's all we do, I'm okay with that. If you tell me that you want me to leave, I'll be disappointed because I just want to be next to you, but I'll do it."

"We can't—I mean, we can't tell people. My sister, if she comes home, will find out, but you're about to be my boss, Spencer."

"Let me worry about that. There are no rules against employees dating."

"I'm sure that's not true of the CEO."

I nod. "Trust me, Charlie girl. I've combed over the employee handbook like my life depended on it since I found out you were working for the practice we were about to acquire. There are no rules. We do this however you want. For now." I add that last piece. I'm fine with letting her take her time to get used to us, but I won't hide this forever. Fuck, I'm so close to having her.

"Just between us while we're at work."

I nod. "For now." I step toward her. She remains still as I spread my thighs so that her knees are between my legs. My palms brace her cheeks as I tilt her head so that I can see into those pretty blue eyes. "Are you going to let me show you now?"

I watch her throat as she swallows hard. "Y-Yes."

I nod and step back. "Stand for me." I offer her my hand, and she takes it, standing from the bed. I reach for the hem of the shirt she's wearing, and I slowly lift. Her arms automatically rise in the air as I pull the shirt over her head. I toss it behind me, not giving a single fuck where it lands.

"If I remember correctly, the Viking did this to start with." Dipping my head, I pull a pert nipple into my mouth. I lap at the hard peak with my tongue before gently sucking. When she buries her hands in my hair and arches her back, giving me better access, I smile.

"And then the scene progresses." I trail kisses up her chest before pulling away and kissing her lips. It's a soft caress, but it still leaves my cock hard and wanting. I'm so hard it's to the point of pain, but that's okay. I'll deal, and jerking off to the memory of tonight will be enough. Because the scene I read about in her naughty romance was all for her.

Tonight is all about her.

Dropping to my knees. I place a hand on each ankle and slowly let my hands climb. I take my time feeling every inch of her soft skin until I reach the waistband of the tiny shorts she's wearing. "We're not going to be needing these," I tell her as I slip my index finger under the waistband and begin to slide them over her thighs.

When the fabric falls to her ankles, she braces her hands on my shoulders without being told and steps out one foot at a time, and I push the shorts to the side. Sitting back on my haunches, I stare at the sexy woman before me. She's in nothing but a white pair of cotton panties that I want to tear from her creamy white skin.

She moves her hands to cover her breasts, but I pull them down. "Don't. Please, don't ever hide from me."

My fingers dance over her ribs and rest on her small hips. "We need to get rid of these," I say, tracing my index finger under the hem of her panties. "Are you attached to them?"

"To my panties?" she asks, confused. "No. I'm not attached."

"Good." My voice is raspy, and my cock is hard as steel as I grip one side of her panties and tear them. I quickly move to the other side, repeating the process, letting them fall to the floor between us.

"Spencer." She half laughs and half scolds me. "I can't believe you just did that."

THE *Kissing* GAMES

"I asked you if you were attached to them."

"I didn't think that meant that you would be tearing them from my body."

"That's what your Viking did," I tell her. "In fact, he was very rough with your heroine."

"They're... not mine. The Vikings, their fantasies are not mine," she says, pausing as I place a gentle kiss just above her pussy.

"They might not be yours, but it was your romance book that you were reading. The genre that you love, and tonight we're going all in. The fiction you fantasize about is about to be your new reality, Charlie girl."

She whimpers, and my cock twitches. "Did you read that scene, Charlie?"

She shakes her head, and I smile. "Do you want to before we get started, or do you trust me?"

"I trust you."

With those three words coming from her, I feel like I'm the king of the fucking world. With one hand on her hip, I take the other and allow my fingers to trace the lips of her pussy. She's already wet and ready for me, and my mouth waters for what comes next. Not able to resist, I lean in, flicking my tongue over her clit, and she moans, a deep sound from somewhere in the back of her throat, and I want to stay right here. Fuck the scene, but I can't do that. This is what I promised her, and I'm a man of my word. Besides, I'll be getting what I want soon enough.

Standing to my full height, I lick my lips, and her eyes watch the trace of my tongue as I taste her.

"Are you getting undressed?" she asks me.

"The Viking only lost his shirt," I tell her.

"We can make our own rules, Spencer."

"Nah, not tonight, baby. We have a script to stick to." My hands rest on her hips and move to squeeze her ass cheeks. "When I lift you, I want you to wrap your legs around my waist and your arms around my neck."

"Okay."

My hands slide back to her hips, and I lift her off the floor. She immediately wraps those long, sexy-as-fuck legs around me, and her arms go around my neck. "Good girl," I praise, just like the Viking did, and she preens.

Her eyes are closed but pop open once we start to move. "What are we doing?" she asks as I move us away from the bed.

"We're about to get to the fun part," I assure her. "Kiss me." The couple in the book were frantic as they devoured each other, and while I want that, I know the woman in my arms is still uncertain about us, about what I'm about to do, so I want her to have this piece of control. I might be telling her what to do, but she's going to set the pace. She's going to determine when this scene really gets underway.

I don't know what I expected, but it wasn't for Charlotte to bury her hands in my hair and fuse her lips with mine. There isn't an ounce of hesitation as her tongue licks at my lips or as she slides inside once I open for her. She takes what she wants. I thought there was no way she could be any sexier, but this, her taking what she wants, what she needs, not hesitating to lead, that's sexy as fuck.

I walk us to the wall and press her back against it while she's still in my arms. I kiss her as if my life depends on it. She rubs her wet pussy over my thankfully still-clothed cock, because I don't know that I would have been able to stop from sliding inside her. It's taking all I have not to reach between us, tear open my zipper, pull out my cock, and demand that she ride me.

That's not what happened in her book.

I need to move this along.

I grip her ass, and she moans into my mouth. Tearing my lips from hers, I pull back enough to stare into her big blue eyes. "Relax your legs," I tell her.

"I'll fall." There's a slight panic in her eyes.

I squeeze her ass. "I've got you, Charlie girl. I promise I'd never let you fall. Trust me. I need you to just relax your legs."

"Why?"

"I'm going to lift you to my shoulders."

"What?" she gasps.

THE *Kissing* GAMES

"I'm going to lift you to my shoulders. You're going to wrap those sexy-as-fuck long legs of yours around my head and rest your back against the wall. Then, you're going to hold on tight, burying your hands in my hair while I worship your pussy." Her entire body shudders. She bites down on her bottom lip, and those bright blue eyes grow dark.

"We—" she starts, but I shake my head, cutting her off.

"Get out of that pretty head of yours, Charlie girl. Just feel. Let me taste you. Let me make your pussy sing for me."

"Shit. You're good at that."

"Good at what?" I kiss the corner of her mouth.

"Talking."

My head tilts back as my laughter takes over. "I'm a man that knows what I want, Charlotte."

"And that's me?"

"You and your sweet pussy. Now. Relax your legs." This time she does as I say, and I lift her by her ass. She moves her legs over each shoulder, and my mouth waters as her pussy sits right where I need her. Her hands comb through my hair, and my cock twitches, thinking about her pulling at the strands as my mouth takes her over the edge.

With my hands on her ass, I tug her closer. My tongue dips out and circles her clit. She gasps, and she grips my hair, spurring me on. I suck her clit, which causes her to moan.

"Spencer—" she calls out for me. Her grip tightens, and she rocks her hips into my face.

Widening my stance to balance us, I devour her. I get lost in her taste, in her. She's everything I always thought she would be, and she's more. It's not just sex. Not with her, but this is what she's willing to give me right now, and that's okay. I have a plan. I'm playing the long game, and I want this woman to be mine, not just for a night, but for a lifetime.

She tugs on my strands, and at the same time, a low, throaty moan falls from her lips. I don't stop. Not until I feel her body quiver, and she calls out my name. When her body slumps, I step back from the wall, place my hands on her back, and carry her to her bed.

I lay her down softly, trailing kisses up her belly. I don't lift my head until I've shown her breasts some attention. When I do, it's to find those baby blues watching me closely. I open my mouth to say thank you, but knowing Charlotte, she's going to think I'm being cocky. I'm not. What just happened between us will be with me for the rest of my life. "How are you feeling?" I ask instead.

"Are you trying to get me to sing your praises?" she asks.

"No, baby. The way you screamed my name and pulled at my hair was all I needed. Not to mention you coming on my tongue. What I mean is, how are you feeling about us? That it was me who gave you the best orgasm of your life."

"The best, huh?" She laughs, just like I hoped she would. "It complicates things."

"It doesn't have to. I want you, Charlotte. The rest are just details."

"Those details are what feed us and put a roof over our heads."

"There are no rules against it," I remind her.

She reaches for the covers, and I move back, letting her climb beneath them. Once she's settled, I move to lie next to her. "I can see that big brain of yours working overtime. Let me help you." I move in close and place a featherlight kiss on her lips. "I want you, Charlie. Not for a night or a weekend. I want you for movie nights and dinner, and I want you when you're in your nest on the couch curled up with a book. I want to be next to you while you read. I want to call you when I have a good day, and I want to be able to vent to you when my day is shit."

"Sounds like you want a girlfriend."

"Yeah, I guess I do, but to me, you'd be more than just my girlfriend. You'd be my everything."

My heart thunders in my chest. "This isn't us, Spencer. We work together, and I refuse for someone to think that I slept my way into my position."

"Charlie, your position was yours before the buyout. No one is going to think that, and if they do, fuck them. We know the truth."

"Can we... slow this down?" She bites down on her bottom lip, her nerves about what she's asked of me shining through.

She didn't say no.

"As slow as you want, as long as you know what I want."

"Me?" she asks. Her voice is so soft I almost miss it.

"Yeah, baby. You." I kiss her again, slowly stroking her tongue with mine. She doesn't seem to mind that she can taste herself on me. "Can I stay?" I sound like a needy fuck, but I'm not ready to go home.

"You want to stay? As in, spend the night?"

"I do."

"Why?"

"Because after all of these years, I got to find out what you taste like, and I'm not ready to walk away from you just yet. I'll be on my best behavior, I promise."

"Do you know how to behave?" she teases.

I slide my hand over to rest on her cheek. "I'll never break a promise to you, Charlie. We can move this as slowly as you want, but please let me stay. I want to hold you. That's it."

"You'll be here when I wake up?"

I nod. "I want to be."

"I know that I should say no. I should tell you that you need to go home and that tonight should never have happened."

"But?"

"I don't want to. I want to know what it's like to sleep in your arms and to wake up the same way." She nods and rolls over, giving me her back.

Not willing to push her further, I quickly strip down to my boxer briefs before I reach over to turn off the bedside lamp, slide beneath the covers, and pull her into my arms. "This," I say, kissing her bare shoulder.

"This what?" she asks. Her voice is so soft I almost miss it. It's as if she's afraid to hear my answer.

"This is what I've been missing." Her body melts into me at my confession.

"What are we going to tell my sister?"

"Tell her we're dating. Tell her that you're mine. I don't care what you tell her as long as she knows that this is happening. However fast or slow you want it to go."

"Maybe you can—" she starts, but I interrupt her.

"No. I'm not sneaking out. I'm not hiding this, Charlotte. You're not some dirty little secret. We're adults, and it's nobody's fucking business but ours."

"She's my sister."

"Which is why we should be honest with her. I know what you're thinking, Charlie girl, and it's not going to happen. I won't change my mind in the light of day."

She's quiet, and I take that as the discussion is over. I close my eyes and bury my face in her neck. It's still hard for me to believe I'm here with her like this. That I get to hold her in my arms all night long. Hopefully, she'll let me make her breakfast, or hell take her and Audrey out. That works for me too. I meant what I said. I'm not going to hide this. Sure, that makes things a little sticky at work, but we'll figure it out. She's worth it.

"Sweet dreams, Spence," she whispers, and my heart flips in my chest.

"Sweet dreams, Charlie girl."

# Chapter FIFTEEN

## Charlotte

I'VE BEEN LYING HERE IN his arms wide awake for about ten minutes. I don't want to move. I don't want my time with him to end. I also don't want to face my little sister. I know she came home last night. She would have called me to let me know otherwise. She couldn't have missed that his car was in the driveway when she got home or that my bedroom door was shut. Audrey is smart.

I don't have guys stay over. In fact, last night was the first time I've ever slept next to a man all night long. I've dated, but nothing serious, and I was always ready to get back to my space. It's not lost on me that I let Spencer into said space and did so without complaint.

"I can hear you thinking," he says before kissing my bare shoulder. The one he spent the entire night snuggled up against. "Morning, baby."

His sleep-laced voice washes over me, and my body heats. What is it about this man that makes me want him... crave him like I do?

"Morning."

"What are we doing today?" he asks, taking me by surprise.

I want to roll over and face him, but I need to brush my teeth. Instead, I try to wiggle out of his hold. "Where do you think you're going?" he asks.

"I have to pee and brush my teeth."

"Kiss me first."

"Did you not hear me say that I need to brush my teeth?" I ask.

"Not yet. I need a kiss."

The next thing I know, he's got me on my back as he settles between my naked thighs. At some point last night, he lost his jeans and is wearing nothing but his boxer briefs. He drops his elbows on either side of my head and softly brushes my hair out of my eyes. "Kiss me, Charlie."

His cock is hard as it rests against my pussy, the hussy that's already wet and aching for him. Instead of arguing, I kiss him. I can't resist him. It's a slow sweet kiss, no tongue, thankfully. When he pulls back, he kisses the tip of my nose and rolls back to the mattress. "Hurry back."

I nod and rush to climb out of bed and scurry to the bathroom. Thankfully, I have an en suite, so I don't have to venture out of my bedroom and face my little sister. Not yet, anyway. I do my business and quickly brush my teeth. I dig around under the sink until I find one of the extra toothbrushes I get from the dentist twice a year and lay it out on the counter for Spencer before I head back to him.

"I laid a toothbrush on the counter for you," I tell him as I make my way to the bed.

"Thanks, babe." He stands and stretches his arms over his head before coming to meet me halfway. His arm reaches out and stops me from walking past as he leans down and places a kiss on top of my head.

I move to sit on the edge of the bed. I don't know what happens next. So, I wait for him to wrap up his business. It's not long before the bathroom door opens. In a few long strides, he's standing in front of me. With his index finger, he lifts my chin until we're eye to eye.

"There she is." He leans down and kisses me. It's slow and deep and does nothing to tamp down my desire for this man. "That's a good-morning kiss," he says, pulling away and standing back to his full height. "What are we doing today?" he asks again.

"Don't feel obligated to stay," I tell him.

"Charlotte." His voice is hard, and I don't want to look at him. "Look at me." I know that if I don't, he's not going to let this go, so I lift my head and meet his eyes. "You are not an obligation." I nod. "Tell me you understand that."

"I understand. I didn't mean it how it sounded, just that you don't have to hang around if you have something to do."

"You, Charlie. You are what I have to do today. I want to spend the day with you."

"You had to have had plans," I tell him.

"Nothing that can't be pushed to the back burner. Picking up dry cleaning, some laundry, mundane things that can wait."

"So you want to hang out?"

He nods. "With you." He tucks my hair behind my ear. "Do you want me to make you breakfast or take you out for breakfast?" he asks.

I sigh. "I'm certain my sister is up and waiting to drill me with a million questions about why you're here and why you stayed with me last night."

He grins. "Then let me get dressed, and we can go answer her questions."

"You don't have to stick around for this," I tell him.

"You and me, Charlie girl. That's how this is going to go, and no hiding outside of work. For now." He slides into his jeans and picks up his t-shirt. He's barefoot, and his hair is mussed from last night's sexcapades. Just looking at him has my heart beating faster.

"Ready?" He holds his hand out for me, and I place mine in his. He pulls me from the bed and hands me his shirt to put on. I should tell him that it's too soon, but I don't want to. I really like this version of Spencer. I know it's a risk, but it's one that I want to take. So I place my hand in his and allow him to help me stand. With our fingers laced together, he leads us to the door, pulls it open, and we make our way down the hall to the kitchen, where I smell coffee.

"Morning, Audrey," Spencer says as we enter the room.

"Well, well, well, Spencer Pennington. When you asked about my big sis last night, I didn't expect to find you parked in her driveway when I got home."

"What? I'm not allowed to spend the night with my girl?" he asks. He lifts our entwined hands to his lips and kisses the back of my hand. My stomach flutters.

"Your girl?" Audrey's eyes are wide as they bounce between Spencer and me. "Since when?"

Spencer turns to look at me. "I've always wanted her," he says softly, "but I wasn't allowed to officially call her mine until last night."

"Charlotte Krause!" Audrey scolds. "You've been holding out on me."

"No, I mean, not really. Things just kind of progressed, and he's hard to say no to." I meet my sister's gaze, and I know she can tell I'm not willing to say more just yet. I'm in deep with this man.

This has my little sister tossing her head back in laughter. "I'm sure the tall, dark, and tatted has something to do with that." She places her coffee cup on the counter, walks around the island, and pulls me into a hug. Spencer surprises me when he wraps his arm, the one that's free, around both of us.

"I want all the details," Audrey tells me.

"Why don't you ladies go sit and talk, and I'll make breakfast," Spencer offers.

"You don't have to do that," I tell him.

He bends and kisses the corner of my mouth. "Let me spoil you."

"Come on, Charlie." Audrey pulls on my arm. "Thanks for offering, Spencer." He grins and nods. "Just yell if you can't find something."

"Any requests?"

"Nah, we're not picky eaters," Audrey answers and tugs on my arm, but Spencer doesn't let go of the other one.

"One more," he whispers as he bends and presses his lips to mine. He smiles, drops my hand, and turns toward the refrigerator to make us breakfast. I keep my eyes locked on him while I focus on calming my racing heart.

Audrey tugs and I follow along behind her to the living room. With the open floor plan, I know he can see us, but I keep my back toward him, sitting in the same spot I was in when he got here last night. Audrey faces me on the opposite end of the couch.

"Spill."

So I do. I tell her about the kiss while we were at the resort and every interaction since then. "Things just kind of happened."

"He's sexy as hell, and I told you all those barbs the two of you used to fire back and forth were a form of foreplay." She grins, wagging her eyebrows.

"It's complicated and scary."

"Okay, let's start with complicated. Sure, he's going to be your new boss, but he said there are no rules against it. He's the CEO, so he would know."

"Yeah, but I don't want to be the center of office gossip."

"Would you be? I mean, really? You're going to be at the practice. Sure, you might have to go to the hospital at times, but you won't be in the same building, and you won't be reporting directly to him."

"Yeah," I agree. It still feels like I'm breaking the rules somehow.

"Okay, and the scared part. Tell me what scares you."

"Oh, you're not going to tell me?" I sass.

"I can. However, it's better if you can admit it to yourself."

"I'm not in denial, Audrey."

"Then tell me. What scares you?"

"What scares me? The way he makes me feel. The way my heart races when he's close. The way I can't stop thinking about him. The fact that he's about to be my boss. I'm scared that if I don't

push him away, he's going to own me heart and soul, and when he decides he's done, I'm going to be crushed."

"He makes you feel, Charlie. That's a good thing. Your heart is racing. That's chemistry. It's necessary. The fact that you can't stop thinking about him, this is more than just a crush, big sister. He's going to be your boss's boss. No rules are being broken. And as far as him pushing you away, there is no guarantee. Look at me. Linc and I were happy. We were ready for forever, but things didn't work out." She shrugs, and I open my mouth to apologize, but she speaks again, stopping me. "It sucked, but it was for the best. We were comfortable. The heart racing, 'constantly thinking about each other' feelings, were gone. Linc is married to his job. I was second, and he was right to call off the wedding. I want more. I *deserve* more. I'm glad that he made that choice for us. I'm not sure that I would have."

"You deserve everything." My eyes mist with tears.

"So do you, Charlotte. We've lost so much, but we can't be closed off to love."

"Who said anything about love?" I ask.

"You're afraid you're going to be crushed if this ends. That's a big *if*. I've known Spencer for a while now, and I've never known him to lead someone on. In fact, I've never known him to be seriously dating someone."

"Yeah."

"The two of you have that in common."

"We do. I'm not sure if that's a good thing or a bad thing. We don't know how this works."

"Oh, come on now. I call bullshit. You watched our parents." She reaches out and takes my hand. "We know what it looks like. I forgot that for a while, but I remember what their love looked like, and I want that for us."

"I want that for us too."

"He asked you out all those years ago. Maybe this is your time? Life is funny like that." She gets a wistful look in her eyes.

"You trying to tell me something?"

"Maybe, but it's too soon. I promise if it's something, you'll be the first to know."

"Okay." I nod. "What about you? He was—*is* Linc's best friend."

"That has no bearing on you and him. Linc and I will get to a place where we can be in the same room together. Spencer is not Linc. If you want him, don't let anything hold you back."

"My little sister handing out life lessons," I say, smiling at her.

"I learned from the best. In the meantime, allow yourself to live and to love. They would want that for you. For both of us."

"Breakfast, ladies!" Spencer calls out.

Audrey gives my hand a gentle squeeze and climbs off the couch. I do the same, following behind her. She immediately starts making herself a plate, but before I do, I go to Spencer and give him a hug.

"Thank you for making us breakfast."

He wraps his arms around me and holds me close. I don't know how long we stand like that, but when he eases his hold, he smiles down at me. "I like taking care of you," he says softly.

"You're going to mess around, and I'm going to get used to this."

"Good."

There is no hesitation. I know my sister is right. I know that I need to just see what happens. I want to see what we can be. I need to stop worrying about heartache and just live. My parents left this earth far too soon, and Audrey and I both owe it to them to live like today could be our last. If it was, I'd want to spend it just like this.

I tilt my head back to peer up at him, and he drops a kiss on my lips. "Come on, let me feed you. I need to run to my place to shower and either grab clothes, or you can stay there tonight, and we can pack a bag for you." Something happens inside my chest. It feels as though my heart is opening up and expanding, adding space for this man. My rival.

"Another sleepover?" Audrey asks. He didn't lower his voice that time.

"I just got her, Audrey. No way am I letting her go that easy."

My sister smiles. "Well, I, for one, vote for you to stay here if this is what every morning is going to be like," she says, taking a hefty bite of her scrambled eggs.

"I'll leave it up to you." Spencer releases me and makes a plate, handing it to me with a smile. "Eat."

"Yes, sir."

His chocolate eyes darken, and I can feel the blush coating my cheeks. I didn't mean for it to be sexual, but who am I kidding? This is Spencer, and he's sex personified. Of course, his mind would go there. Or maybe it's just me.

I take a seat at the island next to Audrey, and Spencer takes the seat next to mine. He places his hand on my thigh, and that's how we eat. Audrey and Spencer talk as if they're long-lost friends, and I guess they kind of are. She was engaged to his best friend, so of course, they know each other well enough to keep the conversation going.

"Thanks for breakfast, Spencer. I need to shower and head out."

"What are your plans today?" I ask her.

"Oh, just doing some shopping. You're welcome to join us."

Spencer squeezes my thigh. "I want to spend the day with you, but if you promise I get you tonight, I'll concede the day."

"Is that you giving me permission?"

"No. You don't need my permission, Charlie. This is me telling you that I demanded to spend the day with you, but if you want to go with your sister and the girls, come home to me. That's all that I ask."

"Damn, Spencer." Audrey whistles, making him laugh.

I look over at the man sitting next to me. He's so open about us, just as he said. He's not hiding. He doesn't care that Audrey heard him. "I want to spend the day with you," I tell him. My voice is softer than his, but I have no doubt that my sister heard me. Her next words prove she did.

"Sounds good. You kids have fun." She waves and rushes down the hall to her room.

"You chose me," Spencer says, leaning in close, his lips hovering over mine.

"I guess I did."

"Mine," he says as our lips touch. The kiss is deliberate and slow, perfect for a lazy Saturday morning. When he pulls back, he watches me for my reaction.

"So, what's the plan?"

"Can we stay at my place tonight? I want you in my bed."

"Yes. I need to shower and pack some clothes. Tomorrow, I'll need to be home to grocery shop and do laundry to get ready for the work week."

"Pack your bag. You can shower at my place."

"With you?"

"Is that what you want, Charlie?"

I nod. He makes me feel bold and empowered. Like I can step out of my structured shell and ask for what I want. What I want right now is to spend the day with him. For the first time since losing my parents, I want something for me, not because of a job or a scholarship. Something all for me, just because I want it, and I want Spencer.

"Anything you want, baby. Go pack a bag. I'll clean up."

"I can help."

"I got this. Go get what you need."

"Thank you for breakfast."

He smacks me on the ass. "Go, Charlie."

I stick my tongue out at him, laughing as I rush to my room to pack a bag.

# Chapter SIXTEEN

Spencer

THE DRIVE TO MY PLACE is quiet. My hand rests on her thigh, and it feels normal. Good. As if we've made this trek from her place to mine hundreds of times. There's an ease between us today that I hope stays with us.

"Here we are," I tell her as I pull into the driveway, releasing my hold on her to hit the button for the garage door opener. "There's an extra bay," I say as I pull inside. "I can hook your car up to it, so when you drive here, you can park inside too."

"That's... a big deal."

"Did you not get the memo, Charlie girl? We're kind of a big deal." Her wide smile lights up her face. She shakes her head as if she's not quite sure what to do with me.

"You're too much."

"But I'm yours." The line is cheesy as fuck, but that doesn't make it any less true. There's also the fact that I've never been this way with anyone I've ever dated. No way in hell would I tell them they could have a spot in my garage, in my home. Everything is different with Charlotte.

Different.

Better.

All-consuming.

"How are you still single, oozing all of that charm?" she teases.

"I was waiting for you." I don't know if that's true, but I do know that no one has ever made me want more. Just Charlotte.

We climb out of the car, and she stops and bends over, pretending to do something with her ankles. "What are you doing?"

Still bent over, she turns her head to look up at me. "Shit's getting deep. I figured I should roll up my pants legs." She chuckles, barely getting her reply out.

"Come on, funny girl." I smile, offering her my hand. I've never seen this side of her before, and I love it. I feel like the real Charlie is here with me, and I want more of her.

"I need to get my bag."

I hold it up. "Already got it."

"You know it's not good to spoil me like this. I might get used to it and start depending on you." There's teasing in her tone, but it also holds something more. Concern, maybe a little fear.

"Good."

"Good?"

"That means I don't have to fight to keep you. I just need to spoil you."

"Fight to keep me?"

"Yeah. I feel like I need to prove myself. To be honest, it's hard for me to wrap my head around the fact that you're here. Too many nights I've sat on that couch"—he points to the couch in the living room—"and thought about our interactions over the years, among other things."

"What kind of other things?" There's a glint of teasing her in eyes. She wants me to say it, and I'm not going to. I'd rather show her.

"Just you, Charlotte."

"Fine. Don't tell me."

"If I have my way, we'll have lots of time for me to show you."

"We have all night," she replies.

"I need more than tonight. You know that, right? This is the long-haul, end game, a game of Monopoly kind of deal."

"Monopoly?" She chuckles.

"You and I both know that a game of Monopoly can go on forever." I watch her as she swallows hard, processing my words. She knows exactly what I'm trying to say. My girl is smart as hell.

"Forever is a long time, Spencer." Her tone tells me she wants to believe me, but she's still not certain.

I drop her bag to the garage floor and pull her into my arms. "I'm not sure even that would be long enough."

"You have to stop that." Her cheeks turn a beautiful shade of pink.

"Stop what?"

"Making me fall harder for you."

"Never." Leaning down, I place my shoulder at her belly and lift her in the air. She squeals with laughter as she smacks my ass. Bending, I grab her bag and start up the stairs. With every day that passes, I watch her walls crumble a little more. Brick by brick, she's allowing me to get close to her, and that's an honor I take seriously.

"I can walk." She's laughing, and the sound bounces off the walls as we make our way upstairs. Less than ten minutes here, and she's putting her mark on my home.

Putting her mark on me.

I don't stop until I'm in my bedroom. I decide we need to shower and save water. We should do it together. I keep going until I'm inside the master bath and placing her sexy ass on the counter.

"Wow. This looks like a spa. And that tub...." Her eyes find mine. "I'm jealous."

"What's mine is yours, Charlie. You can take a bath here whenever you want." It's on the tip of my tongue to tell her that she can move in and take one every single night or day or whenever it suits her, but I bite back the reply. I know I'm coming on strong already. I told myself I would go slow and not push her away, but the more time we spend together, the more I don't know if I can stand by that promise.

"There you go making more promises."

"You want a bath?"

"Maybe." She looks at the tub longingly.

My plans to run my soapy hands all over her body will have to wait. "I'll start it for you. I don't have any bubble bath or any other girly items. You should tell me what you like, and I'll make sure to have it next time."

"Spencer, stop." She lifts her hands and frames my face. "I'm here with you. I want to be here. You don't have to keep up with this nice-guy charm you have going on."

"This is what you do to me, Charlie. I'm not this guy. I don't say all the cheesy lines. I don't invite women to my home, and I sure as fuck don't make them promises. Just you, Charlie girl. You bring this out in me. I'm not playing games with you. I just— I want to give you everything."

"It's kind of fast, don't you think?"

"No. It's been ten years, Charlotte. Ten years ago, I saw you sitting in that auditorium, all this gorgeous auburn hair, and I wanted you. I've wasted so much time on assumptions with you, and I don't want to lose another minute. Never again will I hold back where you're concerned. I'll never not speak my mind. I don't want to lose another ten years of time that I could be loving you." Her eyes widen, and I curse inwardly.

"Spencer—" she starts, but it's obvious that she's having a hard time finding the words.

"Get naked, baby. I'll start your bath." I move away from her, but she reaches out and snags my wrist. I stop and give her my eyes.

"Will you take one with me? It's big enough for both of us, right?"

This fucking woman.

"Yeah, Charlie. It's big enough for both of us." I lean in for a kiss, and she doesn't hesitate to kiss me back. When I finally pull away, my cock feels like a rod of steel behind the zipper of my jeans.

I start the water in the tub, making sure it's warm before I set the plug so it can fill up. I turn back to her, and she's standing naked in front of me. She's shifting from foot to foot, completely unaware that she's the most beautiful creature I've ever laid eyes on.

"Stunning."

She shakes her head as a shy smile pulls at her lips. "You're overdressed, Spence."

She doesn't need to tell me twice. Reaching behind me, I grip the neck of my shirt and pull it off, tossing it toward the hamper. I don't care where it lands. My eyes are locked on hers as I unfasten the button of my jeans and slowly lower the zipper. The sound has her gaze moving to where I'm pulling my jeans over my hips, letting them fall to the floor before I step out of them and my socks all at once.

"Almost," she says huskily.

This is the first time she's going to see me naked, and by the way her stare is glued to my hard cock beneath the tight material of my boxer briefs, she's here for it. Sliding my fingers beneath the waistband, I pull at the fabric, making sure I move the material away from my cock that's growing harder by the second with her eyes trained on me. I get them past my thighs, and they fall to the floor. I step out and kick them away.

"Charlie," I rasp. Fuck me. Her eyes on me have my skin feeling hot all over. Her attention snaps to mine, and her cheeks turn a bright shade of pink. I hold my hand out for her, and she takes small steps toward me, placing her palm in mine. I give her hand a slight tug, and our naked bodies collide. My cock twitches against her belly, and she sucks in a breath.

"That's all for you, Charlie girl." I kiss the top of her head, relishing the feel of this beauty in my arms with nothing between us. "Come on." I take a step back and move to the tub. "Step in." She does so hesitantly and sighs once she's sitting in the warm water.

Without having to tell her, she scoots forward, making room for me. I step in behind her and pull her front to my back. My cock rests against her ass as she leans her weight against me. "I've never used this tub," I confess.

"Really? How long have you lived here?"

"About a year and a half."

"This is a lot of house for a bachelor. Not at all what I expected."

"I bought this place knowing that I one day wouldn't be a bachelor. At least I'd hoped." I move her hair to the side and place my lips against her neck. "What did you expect?"

"I don't know, but not this beautiful home."

"It's a big lonely house," I admit.

"Yeah, my place isn't near as big, but before Audrey moved in, I understood the part about being lonely. I still do. Our lives are so busy, we pass each other coming and going."

"I get that too. When Linc stayed here just for a week, I hardly ever saw him."

She's quiet, and I know her well enough to understand that she's working herself up to asking a question she's not sure she has the right to ask.

"Just ask me," I say, wrapping my arms around her.

"You said you knew one day you wouldn't be a bachelor."

"I did."

"Do you want to get married? Or...." Her voice trails off, not wanting to ask me more, but that's okay. I'll give her more than she asked for.

"Yeah, I want to get married. I wanted the big house, which I've taken care of. Now I just need the love of my life to take my name, so we can fill this big place with babies."

"You want babies?" she asks softly.

"I do. How about you? You ever think about changing your last name and having a few littles calling you mom?"

"It's definitely something I've thought about."

"How many?"

"Kids or husbands?" she asks, and I tickle her side. She squirms, and water sloshes around in the tub. "Just kidding," she says, settling back in her spot against my chest. "At least two. I guess it just depends on my husband. You?"

"This is a five-bedroom house."

"So, three and a guest room?" she asks.

"Four. The guest room is in the basement."

"You want four kids?"

"Why should I deprive the world of these Pennington genes?" I tease.

"They broke the mold with you, Spence."

"Maybe." I laugh. "I was an only child, and it was an all-new level of loneliness. My parents always invited friends on our vacations, and I was always allowed to have a friend over, but it's not the same. Those friends have lives, wives, and kids, and we see each other less and less as the years pass by. If I had siblings, that wouldn't happen."

"What about animals? We were never allowed to have them growing up because our mom was allergic."

"Why not get one now?" I ask.

"Honestly, I'm not sure. At first, it was because I was in college and then starting my new job, which led to buying my first house, and... I don't know. It never seemed like the right time, I guess."

"Dogs or cats?"

"Dogs. You?"

"Dogs."

"Inside or out?" I love this moment with her as we get to know each other on a level that's never been an option for us until now.

"I don't think I have a strong opinion either way. What about you?"

"Well, I'm going to have four kids, so if it's an inside dog, he or she needs to be good with kids."

She turns her head to look at me. "You surprise me, Spence."

"Good surprise?"

"Definitely a good surprise."

We talk until the water runs cold. It's one of the greatest moments, one that I'm certain I will remember and cherish for a long damn time. "We should jump in the shower."

"We're already pruned." She giggles as she holds up her wrinkled fingers.

"It won't take long. We'll shower and then order takeout, or we can see what I have in the kitchen to make."

"Either is fine with me." She moves forward and releases the plug on the tub, and stands. I watch as the water slides over her body. She moves to step out, and I offer her my hand.

"Be careful," I warn. Once she's safely out of the tub, she rushes to the shower and turns on the hot spray. I follow behind her, pulling her back to my front while we wait for the water to heat up.

We take turns washing each other. My soapy hands all over her skin is hot as fuck, but I hold back. I don't want her to think that she's only here so I can fuck her. I want this with her. The more time we spend together not arguing only cements that fact.

I rinse off and step out, while she rinses the conditioner from her hair. I wanted to help her, but I needed to step away to get myself and my cock under control. When she turns off the water and steps out of the open shower, I hold a towel up for her, and she steps in close, allowing me to wrap it around her before handing her another for her hair.

"I'm going to get dressed and head downstairs and see what our options are for lunch."

"Let's just order pizza," she suggests.

"Pizza I can do. What do you want on it?"

"I'm not picky. Just no anchovies."

"Meat lovers?"

"That works for me."

I bend to kiss her. "Take your time."

"We're staying in, right?"

"That was the plan."

"Okay, just making sure. I brought comfy clothes and going-out clothes, and I'm not going to mess with my hair if we're just lounging."

"A day of lounging with you is perfect." I kiss her quickly and leave her in the bathroom to do her thing. I slide into a pair of underwear, some gym shorts, and a T-shirt before making my way downstairs. I call in an order for a large pizza with breadsticks and kick back on the couch.

Just as I get comfortable, there's a knock at the door. Not sure who it could be, I make my way to the door and pull it open. Lincoln stands there with a six-pack of beer and a pizza in his hands.

"Hey, man." He steps past me as I close the door behind him.

"What are you doing here?"

"A man's gotta eat. I thought I would buy lunch as a thank you for letting me stay here when everything went down."

"I just ordered pizza."

He shrugs. "Not like it will go bad."

Before I get a chance to tell him about Charlotte, she steps off the bottom step. She's wearing a tiny pair of shorts that mold to her skin, a tank top that shows her bra strap, and her still-damp hair is pulled up into some kind of twist on top of her head.

"Charlotte— Hi." Lincoln waves.

"Hey, Linc." She's polite and even smiles at him.

"I, uh—" Lincoln is caught off guard, and if it were not for the fact that I don't want Charlotte to feel uncomfortable, I'd let him sweat a little longer.

"Linc, this is my girlfriend, Charlotte," I introduce them as if they're strangers.

Charlotte's eyes widen, as do Lincoln's. I reach for Charlotte, and she comes to me easily. I wrap my arms around her, needing her close.

"I... I didn't know," Lincoln stammers.

"It's new. We've been spending a lot of time together, and we just made it official this weekend." I leave out that work is what brought us together. I know that's still an uncertainty for

Charlotte. Besides, we haven't really discussed labels, so I'm pushing my luck here.

"Wow, congrats, you guys. I'm sorry that I just barged in here like this. I'll just—" He points to the door. "I'll just go."

He takes two steps before Charlotte speaks up. "Linc." He freezes and turns to face her. "You should stay and eat. I can go back upstairs if it makes you uncomfortable."

"No." She's not hiding upstairs. I want her comfortable in my home. She has just as much right to be here as my best friend. Even more so if I'm being honest.

"It's okay, Spence."

"No. He's right. This is your space as his girl as much as it is his."

This is why this man is my best friend. He's made mistakes, but he's a good man. "He's right," I tell Charlotte.

"Look, Charlotte, I'm sorry. I know the way I handled things was wrong, but I really do feel as though it was what was best for Audrey. I'm married to my job, something I need to work on, and she deserved more than I was giving her."

Charlotte nods. "Audrey tells me that there will be a day when the two of you are friends again."

"I hope so." Lincoln bows his head.

I'm floored when Charlotte replies, "Spencer is important to both of us," she tells him, and there's this feeling in my chest. It's one I've never felt before, almost like my heart is bursting open.

"Please stay."

"Are you sure, Charlotte?" Lincoln asks.

"Positive." She turns to me and offers me a small smile, and I will always remember this moment as the one where I fell in love with Charlotte Krause.

# Chapter SEVENTEEN

## Charlotte

I'T'S BEEN REALLY HARD FOR me to concentrate today. Spencer dropped me off at my place last night after we spent all day yesterday together. I didn't get to do my grocery shopping, and my laundry is piled up, but I'm not mad about it. Not even the slightest. This weekend with him was magical. More than I ever could have dreamed.

All I've been able to do since he dropped me off is think about him. About our time together. I'm torn because it feels wrong. We spent so many years arguing, and now here we are, having sleepovers and… more. The more is what causes my face to heat. I don't have to look into a mirror to know. I can feel it. What's worse is that I can feel him. I can hear him and feel his hands on my skin. He's consumed me.

A knock at my door pulls me out of my Spencer haze.

"How are you today?" Dr. Phillips asks.

"Doing well." I don't mention that he just busted me daydreaming about a certain sexy CEO.

"I have some paperwork that needs to go to Spencer. It came back from the bank sooner than anticipated. Would you mind dropping it off to him at the hospital?"

"Sure. I don't mind at all."

"Thanks. It's our most recent bank statement. How's the buyout going? I thought for sure it was going to be a done deal a couple of weeks ago." I can hear the worry in his voice.

"It's going well," I reassure him. "He just wants to get a better idea about the staff given the clause that all jobs are safe outside of new disciplinary action that might occur. He's just covering his bases." I never thought I'd see the day that I would defend Spencer Pennington, but here we are.

"So you think it still looks like this is going to be a go?" he asks.

"Definitely. I think Mr. Pennington is just dotting all of his i's and crossing all of his t's. He's very thorough." Calling him Mr. Pennington doesn't keep me from remembering how thorough he was with me this weekend.

"Good. Good." He seems to be relieved at my reassurance. "Why don't you go ahead and take this over to his office and take off the rest of the day? I appreciate all the support you've provided during this transition."

"Oh, I don't mind coming back," I tell him.

"No. Go, enjoy the early day off. I'll see you tomorrow."

"Tomorrow Mr. Pennington and I are visiting the Calloway and Bridgewater locations to go over staffing files. I believe that's the final piece he's waiting for."

"That's good news. Thank you, Charlotte." He raps his knuckles against my door frame, and walks away.

Grabbing my phone from my desk, I pull up Spencer's contact to send him a text but decide I'll surprise him. Besides, he might be in a meeting, and I don't want to interrupt. If he's in his office, I'll say hello. If he's not, I'll leave the documents and head home. Decision made, I pack up my laptop, grab the envelope and my purse, and head out. It's been a long time since I took half a day. That makes this Monday a lot more bearable.

The drive to the hospital is short, but I'm still sitting here in my car. The air conditioning is on full blast because it's hot as hell outside. I'm second-guessing my decision to surprise him. I could easily leave the envelope with his secretary, Cheryl. I've talked to her on the phone a few times in the last couple of weeks. I don't need to see him.

I want to see him.

Here lies the problem. I'm falling hard and fast for this man, and everything is twisted. I still feel like I'm doing something wrong, even though I know that I'm not. My phone rings and I welcome the distraction from my mental turmoil. I don't recognize the number, so I put on my most professional voice.

"This is Charlotte," I answer, and cringe at how stuck up I sound.

"Charlotte, hi, this is Tabby from Calloway Cancer Center."

"Yes. Hi." I sit up a little straighter in my seat while reaching over to turn the fan down on the air conditioner.

"You applied for our COO position, and we'd like to set up an interview."

"Yes. That would be great. Thank you."

"When are you available?"

"I do have a full-time job, but I can make whatever times work. Unless you have something this afternoon?" I ask hopefully. "I'm off for the day," I explain, trying not to ramble.

"You know what, can I put you on hold for a few minutes?"

"Of course."

Hold music plays in my ear, and I expel a heavy breath. My palms are sweating, and I want to turn the fan back up on the air conditioner. Even the cold blast can't help this. It's my nerves.

The Calloway Cancer Center is a treatment center, and they're in need of a new Chief Operating Officer. It would be a step up from my current administrator position. It's a huge facility. They're their own little mini-hospital treatment center. This is my dream job. COO and CEO, that was always the goal while getting my MBA. I knew the pediatrics practice wasn't my end game, but I've become complacent with my position there. This change, the buyout pushed me to look for another position, and never in my wildest dreams did I imagine I'd get a phone call from the very job I squealed over finding.

I smile, thinking back to finding the job while I was scrolling last night. I'm glad Audrey was in the shower. I haven't told my sister about my job hunt. I wanted to wait to see if I'd get any interest before telling her.

"Charlotte?" Tabby asks.

"Yes, I'm here."

"How is three thirty this afternoon? Our CEO Susan is who you will be meeting with."

"Yes. I can be there at three thirty." I glance in the rearview mirror, and my smile is a mile wide.

"Perfect. When you come into the building, you'll see a reception desk. Just ask for Tabby. I'm the human resources manager. I'll be down to greet you."

"Thank you so much, Tabby."

"You're welcome. I look forward to meeting you."

The call ends, and I do a little dance in my seat. I'm so excited. This is a big deal for me. I want to call my sister, but she doesn't even know I've been looking. My next thought is to tell Spencer. That could solve this constant nagging feeling that I'm doing something wrong. But I don't want to tell him yet either. Not until I know for sure. With a huge smile on my face, I grab the envelope and make my way into the hospital, following the signs to administration.

"May I help you?" a lady with salt-and-pepper hair pulled back into a bun asks me.

"I'm Charlotte Krause. I have some documents for Mr. Pennington," I tell her.

"Oh, Charlotte." She stands from her chair and offers me her hand. "I'm Cheryl. It's so nice to meet you."

"Hi, Cheryl." I shake her hand. "It's nice to put a face to the name." I offer her a genuine smile that she returns.

"Spencer is in his office. You can go on in." She points down a hallway. "His is the last door on the right."

"Thank you, Cheryl." I give her a small wave and head down the hall. When I reach his door, it's open, but he's not alone. There's a woman standing next to his desk. I start to step out of the doorway because I don't want to interrupt him, but he sees me before I can.

"Charlie?" There's surprise in his tone.

Already busted, I walk the short distance to his doorway and step into his office, staying by the door, and wave awkwardly. "Hi." I clear my throat.

"This is a nice surprise." He pushes back from his desk, moves around the woman, and makes his way to me. He surprises me when he bends and places a kiss on my cheek, giving my waist a gentle squeeze before pulling away. "What are you doing here?" He smiles down at me like my visit has made his entire day.

My eyes dart to the woman in the room. He turns to face her, placing his hand on the small of my back. "Lucia, this is Charlotte Krause. She's the administrator of the pediatric practice we're buying," he explains.

"Nice to meet you," Lucia says, her tone telling me it's not nice to meet me at all. "I'll be your boss," she blurts out.

"Lucia is the Director of Physician Services. You will be reporting to her, and Lucia reports to our COO, who is out of town, which is why she's here seeking me out. Right, Lucia?" There is something in the tone of his voice. A warning, maybe? Whatever it is, Lucia's eyes widen, and she nods.

Spencer turns his back to her and gives me his full attention. "What are you doing here, Charlie girl?" he asks softly.

"I have some paperwork for you from Dr. Phillips. He said that you weren't expecting it until later in the week, but he got it today and asked me to drop it off to you."

"Thank you. Have you had lunch? I was just about to go grab something."

"I thought you were too busy to eat?" Lucia pipes up.

Spencer's shoulders stiffen as he turns to look at her. "I think we're done here, right, Lucia?"

Her face turns bright red as she nods and gathers the notebook sitting on the chair next to her. She glares at me the entire time as she walks toward where we're standing just inside the doorway.

"I'm so sorry," I say once she's out of earshot.

Spencer reaches over and pushes the door closed. "There is nothing for you to be sorry about. She's out of line. She's been out of line for weeks, and it was time I nipped that in the bud."

"She's going to know about us."

"Already told you, I'm not hiding anything between us. She was hitting on me. She has been for weeks, hell, maybe months. I've been ignoring her and pretending it wasn't happening, but I'll be damned if she's going to talk to you like that."

"She was simply telling me that she was going to be my boss."

"She was out of line, and it's how she said it. Then she was getting pissy about lunch. I don't have time for lunch with her, but I will always have time for lunch with you." He leans down and kisses me softly. "What do you say? Have lunch with me?"

"I have to be in Calloway around three for a meeting." An interview is a meeting, so I'm not lying. Just omitting some information. I'm not ready to tell him yet.

He looks down at the watch on his wrist. "It's noon. We have plenty of time. I have a one thirty I need to be back for." He kisses me again. "Please?"

"Yeah, let's go have lunch." I can't say no to him.

He grins and walks back to his desk to grab his suit jacket and his phone before reaching into his desk top drawer and grabbing his keys. When he reaches me, he laces his fingers with mine, and I try to pull away, but his grip is firm. "No hiding, baby." He winks, and my belly does a flip. "Not even here. We're doing this."

I'm in so much trouble with this man. I nod, because I don't want to hide anymore either.

He leads me out of his office and down the hallway. We stop in front of Cheryl's desk, and her face lights up when her eyes flash to us, holding hands. "We're going out to grab lunch. Can I pick anything up for you?" he offers.

"Oh, heavens no." Cheryl waves him off. "You two enjoy your lunch. You have a one thirty," she reminds him.

"Got it, boss." He salutes her, making her chuckle.

Hand in hand, he leads me out of the hospital as if it's the most normal thing in the world. It is a casual act, just not for us. Well, I guess maybe it is for the new us. I'm still nervous about the backlash it will cause him and the downfall for me. It's obvious my new boss wants my... Spencer. I really hope I get this job.

That would mean that Spencer isn't my boss's boss and that I could really, truly allow myself to give this a chance. I'm enjoying getting to know this side of him, a side I never allowed myself to believe existed.

"What are you in the mood for?" he asks as he opens the passenger door for me.

"Something fast so you're not late for your meeting." He nods and closes the door, racing around and sliding behind the wheel.

"How's the deli over on Central Avenue?"

"That actually sounds really good. It's been a while since I've been there."

"I go there at least once every few weeks. I like that they have that back seating area that's private. I take my laptop and work while I eat."

"We don't have to do this if you have too much to do."

"I'll always have too much to do, Charlotte. That's part of the job. I run a hospital, but my to-do list will always be growing. I will not put that before you. I'm a smart man, Charlotte. I watched Linc and Audrey. While we all accepted that's just who he is, I don't want to be him. I don't want to wake up in three years and realize I lost precious time with you because I didn't give you more of my time. I spend enough time there, and I'm entitled to lunch with my girlfriend."

"That's the second time you've used that title."

"Is there something else you'd like for me to call you? My book thang, my beau, my partner, my lover, my woman, the ole lady?" He rattles off random ways for him to say I'm his girlfriend.

"Which one is your favorite?" I tease. I honestly can see him using any of them but girlfriend.

"I just want to call you mine, Charlotte. I don't care what title that comes with or how we say it." He reaches over and places his hand on my thigh, and the urge to place mine over his is strong. I stare at his hand as he navigates us through town, and I give in, lacing our fingers together, my hand on top of his.

"I guess we should have that talk, huh? I want you to be my girl, Charlie. I want us to be exclusive, and I want to see where this goes. I feel like we've wasted so much time up until now, and I don't want to waste another second that we could be together."

My heart is racing as I let his words settle inside my chest. "Girlfriend works," I say, my voice hoarse with emotion.

He doesn't say a word until he's parked in the side parking lot of the building that houses the deli. He doesn't let go of my hand as he puts the car into Park, turns off the ignition, unbuckles his seat belt, and turns to face me. "I need to see your eyes when you say it."

"What?" I ask with a soft laugh.

"Your eyes are so damn mesmerizing. They sparkle when you're happy, and I need to see if that sparkle is there. Tell me again."

It feels as though I'm melting inside. Melted chocolate, just like *his* eyes. This time it's me who lifts our joined hands, and I press my lips to his palm. "You, Spencer Pennington, are my boyfriend."

"Fuck." He's over the console, his lips molding with mine, and I'm thankful for the tinted windows. "Just me?" he asks against my lips.

"Just us."

"I like that, Charlie girl. I like it a whole helluva lot." He grins, and it's his eyes that are sparkling. "Let's go grab some lunch. The sooner we get this day over with, the sooner I get you back in my arms." He reaches for his door and climbs out, and I do the same, meeting him in front of his car. He gives me a "why didn't you wait for me" look, and I shrug, making him smile and shake his head.

"Oh, do we have plans tonight?" I ask as he pulls open the door to the deli, motioning for me to go in first.

"Baby, we have plans every night. Every night of forever, just go ahead and pencil me in."

"So needy," I tease. My heart races, and my belly flops at his words. Every night of forever sounds like a damn fine plan to me.

He wraps his arms around me and leads me to the counter. We order our food and then find a nice quiet table in the back. "So, what did you bring me today?"

"Some kind of report from the bank. Honestly, I didn't look at it. Dr. Phillips asked me to deliver it."

He nods. "I'm pretty sure it's last month's numbers."

"Is the buyout still going to go through?" I ask.

"Yes. It's still going to happen." He takes a bite of his sandwich and swallows before he speaks again. "I have a confession."

"We're minutes into this thing, and you're already making big confessions?"

His lips tilt up in a smile. "Smart-ass. But really, I didn't need to go over the staffing."

"What?" I ask, confused, and take a sip of my lemonade.

He shrugs. "I just wanted to spend more time with you. We were finally at a place after all of these years where we were getting along, and I craved that from you. I needed to see what, if anything, would happen, and here we are."

"You must think I'm easy, huh?" I'm only half joking.

"No. Not at all. Charlie, we're still taking this as slow as you want. Honestly, I just needed to know no other man gets to see you, to kiss you and hold you. That's all for me. The rest is just a bonus."

"That goes both ways."

"That's what exclusive means."

"Is this the right thing? Spencer, you're still my boss in the grand scheme of things."

"It's a nonissue." He reaches into his pocket and pulls out his phone. He types at the screen and slides it across the table for me. "That's an email from human resources. I posed the question. I knew you would need reassurance, and I need you." He says it so simply.

"I can't believe you did that." I skim the email, and he worded it so that it wasn't obvious it was the two of us that are in a relationship.

"That's the thing, Charlie. I'm pretty sure there isn't anything I wouldn't do for you."

"That's getting deep, Pennington." I wait for the nerves to kick in, but it never happens. Spencer has succeeded in tearing down all the walls around my heart.

"We've been dancing around this"—he motions between the two of us—"for far too long. I'm tired of moving in circles. I'd rather be slow dancing with you in my arms."

"What do I say to that?" I ask, feeling all tingly inside. That's what this man does to me.

"Just say you're mine, Charlie. Give us a real chance. The rest will fall into place."

"You sound so certain." Even as I say the words, I know he's already cemented himself inside my heart.

He just grins and takes a bite of his sandwich. For the rest of lunch, we talk about our plans for that night. He wants me to come to his place, but I decline and explain that I need to spend some time with my sister. There is so much going on that I need to catch her up on. He pouts but doesn't complain. All too soon, we're pulling back into the hospital parking lot, and he's walking me to my car.

"Be safe," he says, pulling me into a hug.

"I will."

"I'll call you later."

"Sounds good. Bye, Spence." I move to step out of his arms, but he hauls me back in and kisses me softly. Just a nice gentle peck on the lips, but it still has me wanting more. More that I don't have time for.

He eventually lets me go and steps away. As I'm pulling out of the lot, he stands there watching me. Reaching down, I pinch my leg. The pain smarts, which means I'm not dreaming.

How is this my life?

I'm smiling as I walk into the house. The interview was great. I loved the CEO, Susan. The job is exactly what I always dreamed I'd end up doing. It didn't feel like an interview. I was comfortable, almost as if I was catching up with an old friend. Susan and I would be working closely together, and that connection is important, and we had it. She smiled the entire time, and we even ended up talking about books when she asked me about my hobbies. Turns out she reads romance too, and we compared notes on some of our shared favorites.

"Hey, you. I was starting to worry," Audrey says when she sees me.

"Hi." I smile at her.

"You're super smiley tonight. Good day?" she asks, giving me a smile of her own. She's plating up what looks like grilled chicken salads. "You're just in time for dinner." She nods to the extra plate.

"I did have a good day." I take a seat at the island next to her and add some dressing to my salad. "Thanks for dinner." I take a bite and contemplate how to tell her everything that's been going on in my life and decide to just let it all out, kind of like ripping off a Band-Aid. "I only worked half of the day. I had lunch with my boyfriend and an interview this afternoon for my dream job."

She coughs and stops her fork to her plate. I reach over and pat her back. Her wide eyes find mine. She stares at me for several long seconds before reaching for her drink and taking a huge gulp. "Care to run that by me again?"

I grin. She's certain she heard me wrong. It's not often I have news that can shock people, let alone my sister. Doing as she asks, I repeat my words. "I only worked half of the day. I had lunch with my boyfriend and an interview this afternoon for my dream job."

"Charlotte." Her voice is scolding, and I grin wider. When she sees that I'm not taking any of it back, she turns her stool to face me, and I do the same, looking her in the eye so she can see my truth. "Let's unpack this, big sister." She shakes her head. It's easy to see she's confused and not sure if she should believe me or not.

"You only worked half the day? That's not like you."

"Yep. Dr. Phillips needed me to drop some documents off at the hospital and told me to take the rest of the day off."

She nods. "All right, what about the next part? You had lunch with your boyfriend? How is that going? Are you in looove with him?" she fires.

I feel a tad bit guilty that I've kept what's been happening from her, but it was a whirlwind, and she's been dealing with her own life issues. "Yeah," I tell her. "I had lunch with my boyfriend. Things are going well. It's been kind of a whirlwind, but I wouldn't change it. I was fighting it—this connection that we share. Am I in love with him?" I pause. "I should probably tell him that first."

"Are you seriously going to hold out on me?"

"I need to tell Spencer first." I pause, waiting for her reaction. He is her ex-fiancé's best friend.

"Knew it!"

"Stop. You did not."

"I called it, *Charlie*." She emphasizes the nickname. "All that banter was foreplay."

I shrug. I'm still not sure, but I do know the possibilities of what we could be is keeping a smile on my face. "Maybe."

"And you had a job interview for your dream job? With Spencer?"

"No."

"Start talking, big sister."

So I do. I start from the beginning. I remind her how he asked me out in college and our rivalry. I tell her about the kiss at the resort and then finding out he's going to be my new boss, what happened at the bar after she left, and everything else. I don't leave out a single detail. I pick up my glass and take a drink once I'm done, giving her time to process everything I just told her. It doesn't take long. I barely have time to take a drink when she replies.

"Hell yes, Charlotte! I love this for you. I love him for you. Spencer is a great guy. I tried all these years to tell you that."

"You knew a different version of him."

"And now?"

I nod. "He's a good guy."

"I don't need to ask if he makes you happy. I can see it written all over your face."

"He's my boss. Well, he might not be much longer if I get this job."

"Tell me about the job."

I tell her about my interview and how excited and hopeful I am that the job is mine. "That's really my biggest reservation of giving everything I am to this thing with Spencer."

"You mean your boyfriend. Your relationship."

"Yeah, that." We both laugh at my reply.

"You'll get the job, Charlotte. There is no way they'll pass you up. And you've already got the man. I'm so happy for you."

"I really like him," I confess softly.

"He's crazy about you."

"What?" I ask, raising my brow. "You can't know that."

"He watches you, Charlotte. He's always watched you. When you're not looking, he is. I have a good feeling about this. Wedding bells and all the things." She smiles.

"I'm sorry."

"Hey, you have nothing to be sorry for. I want you to be happy. Linc made a hard choice, but it was the right one. This thing with you and Spencer is separate. And when it's time for me to stand at your wedding, and Linc is there, even if I have to walk down the aisle with him, it will be okay. I don't hate him. I probably should, but I don't have it in me. I'm thankful he ended things. Sure, I wish it would have been sooner, but everything happens for a reason."

"What's that look in your eye?" I ask her.

She shrugs. "I'm not ready to talk about it, but when I am, you are the first person I'll come to."

"I love you, Audrey."

"I love you too."

THE *Kissing* GAMES

# Chapter
## EIGHTEEN

*Spencer*

MY HOUSE IS QUIET. TOO damn quiet. She was here for not even forty-eight hours, and already this place isn't the same without her. Something else that's not the same? My ability to sleep. I can smell her on my sheets, and my arms ache to hold her. It's Thursday night, and I've not laid eyes on her since Monday.

Monday night, she had a night in with her sister. Tuesday night, they went to a yoga class. I begged her to let me come and watch. She declined, so she's going to have to do it here so I can watch. I'll do what I can to convince her.

Last night she had a doctors' meeting. They meet after hours to keep from taking away from patient appointments. I get it. I think it's a great idea, and I'm impressed that they're that focused on patient care to not want to take that time from them. They're also keeping me from my girl, so I'm a little salty, but if I take Charlotte out of the equation, I commend them.

That brings us to tonight. She's coming to my place tomorrow after work. I convinced her to spend the weekend with me, but she countered that she needed tonight to do laundry because she's not been able to catch up this week from being at my place all last weekend.

I can't go another night tossing and turning. I need sleep. I need Charlotte, so that's why I'm here right at six with two pizzas and an overnight bag, and tomorrow's suit tossed over my shoulder. She can't come to me, but I can come to her. I don't know how she's going to take it. There's a good chance she's going to tell me to take my ass home, but I won't know unless I try. My hands are full, so I use my elbow to hit the doorbell.

The door opens, and it's Audrey who greets me. "Fancy seeing you here." She grins.

"I brought dinner," I tell her as I hand her the pizzas. Charlotte told me that she informed Audrey about the details of our relationship earlier this week, and she's team Spencer and Charlotte. Not that I thought she wouldn't be after I made her breakfast. My cooking skills are on point. I'm thankful. It was hard enough winning over one of the Krause women. I couldn't imagine having to convince both of them I'm what's best for her. I'd do it, but I'm thankful that I don't need to.

"She doesn't know you're coming, does she?"

"Nope." I hope they haven't had dinner yet.

"We were just discussing what we were going to have for dinner. You're right on time."

"Perfect."

Her eyes flash to my overnight bag and suit, but she says nothing. She doesn't need to. The smirk pulling at her lips says it all. "Come on in, Spence." She steps back and allows me to enter. "She's in her room. She's in the shower."

Now it's me who smirks. I drop a kiss on her cheek and take off down the hall. I knock on the door, but there's no answer. Trying the knob, I find it unlocked. Of course it is. This is her home, and the only one here is her sister. At least, that's what she assumes. The shower is going, and I grin. Quickly, I strip out of my clothes, rush over to the door, and turn the lock before sneaking into the bathroom. Her shower isn't as big as mine at home, but we'll fit. I pull back the curtain, and she yelps. Her mouth drops open when she sees me.

"Hey, Charlie girl." I wrap my arms around her, hauling her into my chest.

Her arms slip around my waist as she smiles up at me. "What are you doing here?"

"I missed you." I kiss the corner of her mouth. My hold on her tightens just a little. It's damn good to have her in my arms where she belongs.

She pushes my wet hair out of my eyes. "You look tired. You okay?"

"I'm not sleeping."

"What's going on?"

"My bed smells like you. My house is too fucking quiet, and I can't find a comfortable position without you in my arms."

She sags into me. "Spence."

"I brought pizza," I tell her. "And I brought an overnight bag. I was hoping you'd take pity on me and let me stay."

She watches me, and with each second that passes, my heart rate increases. I'm ready to drop to my knees to beg or wear her out with my tongue, whichever comes first, to convince her to let me stay.

"I missed you too," she finally confesses.

My shoulders relax, and I kiss her. For real this time. Not just a peck. I kiss her with everything I have in me. Damn, I really fucking missed her. Miss this, being with her. My cock is hard, but I ignore it. It's something I've gotten used to when Charlotte is around. I can't even imagine a lifetime when I don't want her with this intense ferocity.

"Pizza's getting cold," she mumbles against my lips.

"I like cold pizza," I say, trailing kisses over her neck.

She chuckles. "I'm starving, and as much as I want to see where this will go, you're exhausted."

"I was tired. I'm not anymore."

"Come on, funny man. I'm finished. You do your thing. I'm going to get out and get dressed. I have to swap over my laundry.

I only have one more load. Audrey worked from home today, and she did hers and then started mine."

"Remind me to thank her. That's more time with you in my arms."

"I thanked her, and I was buying her dinner tonight."

"Glad I could take care of that for both of you." I kiss her again and let her go. "Can you grab my toiletries kit out of my bag that's sitting on your floor?" I ask her. "I was too eager to get to you to bring it in here with me."

She gives me a soft smile, one that I cherish. "Yeah. I'll be right back." She kisses under my chin and pulls back the curtain before stepping out.

I keep the curtain peeled back so I can watch her as she dries off, wrapping a towel around her hair and then her body before walking out to get my toiletries. When she steps back into the bathroom, she chuckles at my head sticking out of the curtain.

"Thanks, babe," I tell her when she hands me what I need for my shower.

"You're welcome." Her blue eyes are sparkling and, regardless of my exhaustion, that makes me smile and damn glad she didn't kick my ass to the curb.

I rush through my shower, and when I step out of the bathroom naked as the day I was born, her room is empty. Part of me is relieved because I am utterly exhausted, but the other part, the bigger part, wanted her naked and waiting for me on her bed. That's a fantasy I'll have to table for another day. Besides, we have time. Lots of time if I have anything to say about it.

Pulling on my underwear, shorts, and a T-shirt, I open the door and go in search of my girl and dinner. I find Charlotte and Audrey in the living room. The pizza boxes are sitting on the coffee table. A small stack of paper plates and napkins is next to them.

"I grabbed you a beer." Charlotte points to the beer sitting on the end table.

"Thank you." I bend over and drop a kiss on top of her head before making myself a plate. I don't sit on the opposite end of the couch where my beer is waiting. I've been away from her enough this week. So I take the middle couch cushion, placing myself right next to her.

"This is nice to see," Audrey comments. "To be honest, I wasn't sure either of you would ever get here."

"What do you mean?" I ask her.

She shrugs. "You were both so closed off. I guess it just goes to show the right person makes a world of difference."

"Is it okay that I'm here?" I ask. I know things are weird with what happened between her and Lincoln.

"More than okay, Spencer. This is Charlotte's house, and even if it were mine, I'd feel the same way. Linc's decision has nothing to do with you. Like I told my sister, he made the right choice. I don't hate him. It's going to take me some time, but we'll get to a place where we can be in the same room together and not feel guilt and loss." She takes a long pull of her own beer.

"Thanks again for doing my laundry today," Charlotte tells her sister.

"That's what we do." Audrey shrugs. "I was here anyway, and I know you didn't get to do it last weekend."

"That's on me." I lean over and press a kiss on her shoulder. "Sorry, babe."

"Aw," Audrey coos.

We all laugh. I grab a couple more slices of pizza and listen as the sisters talk about a book they're reading. Once I'm finished, I lean my head on Charlotte's shoulder, and her scent surrounds me. Fuck, how am I already this addicted to this woman?

"I think we're losing him." Audrey chuckles.

"It's your sister's fault. She let me sleep next to her two nights in a row and then took herself away from me. I've slept like shit this week."

"You're a good man, Spencer Pennington," Audrey comments. "I'm going to clean up. You two head to bed before we have to try and carry him to your room."

"I can help," Charlotte tells her sister.

"It's some paper plates, a couple of empty beer bottles, and a pizza box that will get shoved in the fridge. I've got this. You crazy kids behave." She points her fingers at us.

Charlotte stands from the couch and holds her hand out for me. I place mine in hers, and she yanks to help pull me from the couch. We say goodnight to Audrey before she leads me down the hall to her room. We head to the bathroom and brush our teeth before flipping off the bathroom light and moving toward the bed.

"Naked," I tell Charlotte as I push my shorts and boxer briefs over my thighs. I let them fall at my feet and step out of them before adding my shirt to the pile. "I need to feel your skin against mine."

"What if I get cold? You know the air conditioning is chilly at night."

"Naked, in my arms. I promise you, baby, you won't get cold." I climb under the covers and wait for her. I watch her as she slowly strips out of her shorts and tank top before taking her spot next to me. Reaching over, she turns off the lamp, and the room is bathed in darkness.

"Come here, Charlie girl." She doesn't hesitate to slide across the mattress and rest her hand and her cheek on my chest. I wrap my arm around her and hold her close. "This," I whisper. "You," I amend, "are what I needed."

Her hand begins to roam over my chest. "I'm afraid to get too used to this," she says, her voice soft.

"Why?"

"I've never really had a serious relationship, Spencer. I've dated here and there, but nothing that had me craving more. I've never missed anyone the way that I miss you."

"That makes two of us."

We're quiet as she continues to explore. Her hand slides lower and lower until she's gripping my hard cock in her small hand. "Charlie—" Her name from my lips is a warning. Not because I'm exhausted but because I want her with a ferocity that I don't understand.

"Is this okay? Can I?"

I'm not an idiot. I will never tell this beauty that she can't touch me. "As long as it's you." I lift my head to press a kiss to hers.

"Just me."

"Just us," I counter. I can imagine she's smiling and that her blue eyes are lit up from our whispered confession.

She strokes me slowly. Her soft hand pumps from base to tip, circling the head of my cock, repeating the process over and over again. I'm so fucking hard. I want so many things at this moment, but what I want more than anything is to see what she's going to do next. More than that, I want her to grasp the fact that I'm hers and she can do with me as she pleases.

When she shimmies under the covers, I fist her pillow, because I have a pretty good idea what my girl is up to. My cock twitches in her palm at the thought of her sweet lips wrapping around me.

The cover is pulled back, and I look down at her resting between my thighs on her belly. I can't see her eyes, but I imagine the blue is dark and filled with desire like I know my own brown are as they gaze at her. "Is this okay?"

I swallow hard. "I'm yours, Charlotte. You never have to ask for permission to touch me. I can guaran-fucking-tee that anything you want to do is more than okay with me."

"So I don't have to ask to do this?" She slides her hand to the base of my cock, and at the same time, her tongue peeks out and swirls around my head.

"N-No."

"Or this?" She lifts up and takes the head of my cock into her mouth, swirling her tongue in a move that has me gripping her pillow with one hand and the sheets in the other.

"I'm yours," I tell her again.

"Then I definitely don't need permission to do this." The next thing I know, my cock is sliding into her mouth. She can't take all of me, but it's enough.

She is enough.

Over and over again, her head bobs as she sucks my cock. She uses her hands and her mouth, and I have to fight to keep my eyes open. I want to close them and just relish in what she's doing to me, that this beautiful woman is moaning around my cock.

However, I also don't want to miss a single fucking second of my cock in her mouth. Stretching my arm out, I manage to pull the string on the bedside lamp to light the room with a soft glow. I can feel myself getting close, and she moans, and it's time to change things up.

"Ch-Charlie, baby, come here."

My cock falls from her mouth with an audible pop. "What did I do?"

"You're about to make me come."

"Spence, that's the mission here," she says, and I can hear the humor in her tone.

"Yeah, but that breaks the rules."

"What rule is that?" she asks as she strokes me gently.

"The one where I never come before or without you."

"Oh, I think I might like this rule."

"Too bad if you don't. It's here to stay. Now come up here." She does as I ask. "On your knees facing the foot of the bed." Again, she turns on her knees to face the foot of the bed. "Now straddle my chest." I expect complaint, but the only thing I get is compliance. Once she's straddled over me, I can feel her wet pussy pressing against my chest and my mouth waters.

She leans forward, her tits pressing against my belly, and sucks my cock into her mouth. I laugh. I can't help it. She's perfect. "Move back," I tell her.

She wiggles that fine ass of hers until she's where I want her. My hands grip her hips as my tongue dips in for my first taste of her in days.

"Spencer," she breathes, her hot breath ghosting over my cock.

I smack her ass gently, and she moans. The vibration of the sound pulses around my cock, and I'm close. So fucking close. I need her to come. Now. I double my efforts, sucking on her clit. Her legs start to quiver, and I know she's exactly where I am, on the edge of ecstasy.

She moans again, and I can't hold back. I pull away from her and tap her thigh. "Baby, I'm close," I warn her.

My cock falls from her mouth long enough for her to tell me not to stop before she gets back to work, racing me to the finish line. I want her to come with me, so I do the same. I'm not holding back. She takes me deep into the back of her throat, and this time I'm moaning as I spill down her throat. She swallows what I give her before I fall from her mouth, only for her to call out my name. It's not a loud cry, but it's my name on her lips as pleasure rolls through her.

She moves to take her spot next to me, the one that will forever belong to her, and snuggles in close. I wipe my mouth with the back of my hand before wrapping both arms around her. I can't get her close enough. I'll never be able to be close enough to satisfy my need for her.

"Night, Spence."

I smile. "Night, Charlie girl."

It's not long before we're both carried away to a night of rest. She's definitely what I was missing. I just need to figure out how to make nights like tonight permanent for us.

# Chapter NINETEEN

*Charlotte*

MY SISTER IS DATING SOMEONE. At least, I think she is. She's smiling all the time, and she's been home less and less. Not that I can say anything. I'm hardly ever here either, and when I am, Spencer is here with me. After the night he showed up, stating he hadn't been sleeping without me, we've not slept a night apart since.

That was two months ago. During that time, I've had two more interviews with the Calloway Cancer Center, and I was told they would be making a final decision at the board meeting that happened last night. I've been on pins and needles all day waiting, hoping for a phone call.

I still haven't told Spencer. I didn't feel like I needed to unless there was something to tell. I am certain that even if this job doesn't come through, I'm going to keep looking. I don't want others to assume I slept my way to the top, and if I'm being honest, Lucia, my new boss, the one who wants my boyfriend, we don't get along all that well. I don't think she knows about us, but the suspicion is there, and she's mean.

The buyout has been final for the last six weeks or so, and while I still feel like I'm breaking the rules dating the boss's boss, I no longer let it eat at me. That's because I fell in love with him. Yeah, I went from kissing my rival to giving myself to him heart and soul. He owns every piece of me, well, not every piece. For some reason, Spencer keeps putting us sleeping together on the back burner. There isn't a place on our bodies that the other hasn't touched, but he's never been inside me. Well, his cock has never been inside me. I know he's trying to take things slow, but the wait is killing me.

I want him.

I'm in love with him.

It's time.

My desk phone rings, pulling me out of my thoughts. "This is Charlotte," I answer.

"Charlotte, where are we with hiring a new nurse for triage?" Lucia asks. Snarks is more like it.

"The ads are up online, as well as in the paper. You just gave me the go-ahead to post the job three days ago," I remind her. Of course, my tone is kind, not that she deserves it.

"Get it done." The line goes dead, and I roll my eyes.

"Who was that?" I hear a familiar voice. I look up to find Spencer standing just inside my doorway.

"Hey. What are you doing here?" Not that I'm not happy to see him. I just wasn't expecting him.

"I had a meeting that got canceled, and I thought we could go to lunch."

I glance down at the clock on my computer and see that it is, indeed, lunchtime. "I can't believe it's lunchtime already," I tell him as I stand, grabbing my phone and purse. "What happened to the lunch we packed you this morning?" I ask, keeping my voice low.

"Not passing up time with you, Charlie girl." He smiles, and my heart melts. Just like it does anytime this man is near me.

"I'm already yours," I whisper. "You don't have to charm me."

"Damn right you're mine." He slaps my ass, just a love pat really, but it still shocks me. Luckily, we are both still in my office. I really need a different job. I have no desire to be the gossip at the water cooler.

"I still can't believe you planned a picnic," I tell him. He drove us to the deli on the edge of town, the one that seems to be our go-to place. Instead of grabbing our usual table in the back, Spencer asked them to make our food to go and drove us to the park. The weather is not sweltering, but it's a warm fall day here in Charleston.

"I'm very romantic," he counters cheekily.

"I know you are. I live with you, well, I mean not really." I wave my hands in the air, flustered. "You know what I mean."

"You could, you know. If you wanted to."

I have to focus on swallowing the drink of lemonade and not choke as his words register. "I don't know that we're ready for that, Spencer."

"We spend every night with each other. We don't sleep without the other next to us. How are we not ready?"

I bite down on my bottom lip. "Because there are still things we haven't shared, and maybe you might change your mind."

His forehead wrinkles in confusion. "What the hell are you talking about?"

I exhale loudly. Might as well just put it out there. "Sex, Spencer. I'm talking about sex. We've been dancing around it for months."

"Because that's not what this is." He motions between the two of us. "I needed you to know that."

I let his reasoning sink in. "I still think that we should have... done that before we talk about moving in together. Sex changes things."

"Not us."

"You don't know that."

"I do know that."

"Spencer." I sigh.

"No. I know what's going on in that pretty head of yours, Charlie, and you're wrong, baby. You're dead wrong. Sex is not going to change us, at least not the way that you think that it's going to. It's only going to bring us closer together."

"You can't be sure."

"I'd bet my life on it." I squeal when he reaches over and tugs me onto his lap. "You feel that?" He shifts his hips so that I can feel his hard cock pressing against my ass. "That's just because I'm sitting next to you. Every fucking time, Charlotte. I crave you. There will never be a day that I don't want you next to me. When we make love, that's only going to make those feelings grow."

I want to tell him that I'm in love with him. I want to tell him that I feel the same way, but I was worried that he wouldn't. However, there's still something I'm keeping from him. I won't tell him how much I love him until there are no secrets between us. I feel as though I know Spencer well enough to understand that he's going to be disappointed that I didn't share that part of my life with him. He would have supported me through this process. I know he would have. I also wouldn't put it past him to reach out and put a good word in for me. But I want this for me. I want to know that I'm the one who got me this job. Not my CEO boyfriend. The man who owns my heart.

"Charlie?" His arms that are enclosed around me tighten just a little.

"Okay."

"Okay," he repeats.

"I'm not saying never. I just... a little more time."

"I can give you as much time as you need, baby. I just need you in my arms at night, your place or mine. I don't care. We'll work it out when you're ready."

I wrap my arms around his neck and hug him back. "Thank you for putting up with me."

"Was that our first fight?" he asks.

"What? No, we used to fight all the time."

"Not since you've been mine."

I think back to the last couple of months, and he's right. "It was more of a discussion than a fight."

"So, no makeup sex?" he teases.

"Is that what it's going to take? If that's the case, I can start a fight." I tap my index finger against my chin as if I'm trying to decide what fight I could start.

"No." He laughs. "I just wanted to be certain that you knew that us being together had nothing to do with me needing to be inside you."

Heat pools between my thighs at his words. "I'm glad we got that cleared up," I tell him. I move off his lap and cross my legs, hoping the ache he's caused subsides. I still have to go back to the office and work the rest of the day.

"My place or yours tonight?" he asks, picking up his sandwich.

"Doesn't matter to me. I don't have anything that has to be done at home."

"My place then?"

"Sure. I just need to stop by and grab what I'll need for work tomorrow."

"You do that, and I'll start dinner. Will you be home by six?" he asks.

"I can be at your place by six."

"Yeah, home by six." He winks, and I can't help it. I smile. *Smug bastard.*

We finish our lunch and clean up our trash before Spencer drops me off at the office. He leans over and kisses me goodbye, and I'm thankful for his tinted windows. "See you tonight, Charlie girl," he says softly.

"Thanks for lunch." I blow him a kiss as I climb out of his car.

I've just pulled out of the parking lot, heading home to get what I need to stay at Spencer's, when my phone rings. I glance at the screen and see that it's the call I've been waiting on all day. This is it. I slowly inhale as I hit Accept on my steering wheel. "Hello," I greet Tabby.

"Charlotte, hi. It's Susan."

My heart jumps in my chest. It has to be a good sign that Susan is calling me herself, right? "Hi, Susan."

"I know you were expecting a call today, and I'm sorry it's so late. Is now a good time?" she asks.

"Yes, now is good." I signal and pull over to the parking lot of the grocery store and place my car in Park. I know my concentration won't be what it needs to be while I'm on this call.

"I wanted to be the one to call you, and my day got away from me. Anyway, I'm calling to offer you the position of Chief Operating Officer for Calloway Cancer Center." She goes on to tell me the pay, which is a significant increase to my current salary as well as the rest of the benefits package. "If you need the weekend to think about it."

"No," I rush to say, and force myself to take a calming breath. "No. I would like to accept the position. There is nothing to think about. This is an incredible opportunity, and I'm so incredibly grateful that you're taking a chance on me."

"Excellent. Trust me, Charlotte, we are the lucky ones. We are very fortunate that you applied. The board, as well as I, agree that you are a perfect fit for our organization."

"Thank you so much."

"Now, I'll have Tabby call you tomorrow to work out a start date, background check, drug test, and all of that."

"Thank you so much, Susan."

"We'll talk soon," she says, and the call ends.

I sit in my car with a smile on my face, fighting back the tears. I busted my ass in college. I didn't party or stay out too late. I worked two part-time jobs and studied my ass off to make the grades to keep my scholarship.

Closing my eyes, I swallow back the lump in my throat as I think about my parents. I know they would be proud of me, proud of me and Audrey for the lives we're building for ourselves. I wish they were here. I wish I could tell them about this. How I just landed my dream job, and that the guy who I thought was my rival turned out to be my heart.

"I love you," I whisper. I don't know if they're watching over us, but I'd like to think that they are, and they can hear me.

Once I have myself together, I put the car in Drive and head home. The journey is quick, and when I see my sister's car in the driveway, I smile. I can't wait to share this news, and then tonight, I have to tell Spencer. I just hope he understands my need to make sure that I did this on my own. I hope we can get past this. I have faith that we can, and when we do, I want to tell him what he means to me. I want to tell him that I've fallen madly in love with him. I want to finally feel as though I can stop holding back and let this relationship of ours take flight. I want to see where we can go. All the images in my head lead to forever, and I really hope that he's on the same page, or at least the same chapter as me.

I don't bother pulling into the garage since I'm leaving again. I do grab my purse and phone and head inside. "Audrey!" I call out.

"In my room!" she calls back.

Kicking off my heels, I toss my purse and phone on the couch and start down the hall. I knock on her door, and she tells me to come in before I push it open. "Hey." I smile at her.

"Have you been crying?" she asks.

I nod. "Yeah, but I'm good. I promise. Happy tears." I point to my eyes that are once again welling up.

"Oh! Did Spencer propose? Let me see the ring," she demands.

I toss my head back in laughter. "No, Spencer did not propose. We're not there yet."

"You're not there yet. That man would change your last name in a hot minute if he thought you would be okay with it."

"Huh," I say, stepping into the room and sitting next to her on the bed. "Funny, because I would totally be okay with it."

"Seriously? Who are you, and what did you do with my sister?"

"Stop." I lean my shoulder into hers. "I love him, Audrey."

"I know you do."

"I haven't told him yet. I'm a shitty girlfriend that I tell my sister before I tell him."

"I'll pretend like I don't know," she says with a chuckle.

"I got the job," I tell her.

"What?" she screeches as she jumps off the bed. "Charlotte!" She grabs my hands, pulls me to my feet, and crushes me in a hug.

"I'm so fucking proud of you. Mom and Dad would be so proud of you," she says, her voice filled with emotion.

"I hope you know they would be proud of you too."

She nods, then pulls back. "So, the happy tears?" she asks.

"Yeah, the happy tears."

"When do you start?"

"I don't know. The CEO, Susan, called me herself. Human resources is supposed to contact me soon to work out all the other details. It's a huge pay raise, vacation time, and every benefit you could ask for. This is what I always wanted to do."

"It's funny how things have a way of working out," she says.

"Definitely." I tug her into another hug. "I'm staying at Spencer's tonight."

"How did he take the news?" she asks.

"He doesn't know."

"That you got the job or that you applied and got an interview?"

"That." I point at her, feeling the guilt wash over me.

"Charlotte! You haven't told him? He's going to be blindsided."

"I know. I just—I wanted to get this on my own. I didn't want him to make a phone call or write a letter. I wanted them to want me for what I can offer them."

"How do you know he would have done either of those things?"

I shrug. "I guess I don't know for sure, but I know Spencer, and if he thinks that I want it, then he's going to do whatever he can to help me get it. It was that or try to talk me out of it, and I don't want to be the woman who slept her way to the top. Besides, my boss, Lucia, hates me because she wants my Spencer."

"He only has eyes for you," she assures me.

"I know," I admit.

"He loves you."

"I hope he still does after he learns that I kept this from him."

"It's going to take more than this for him to let you go. In fact, I'm not sure there is anything that you could do to make him not want you."

"This is the last and only thing," I tell her. "No more secrets. It's been stressful and hard to keep this from him. Every interview I wanted to call him, but I talked myself out of it."

"I'm going out tonight, but if you come home and need me, or if you need me at all, just text me."

"Hot date?" I ask her.

"Nah, just a group getting together for dinner." Her eyes tell me a different story, but I can't dwell on her secrets right now. It's time for me to go spill my own.

THE *Kissing* GAMES

# Chapter TWENTY

## Spencer

As I RUSH AROUND MY house, setting everything up, I can't help but smile. I left work early. Not just sneaking out of the office a little before five, but I left at three. I couldn't concentrate after my lunch with Charlotte. The fact that she thought I didn't want her was laying heavy on my mind. I could see it in her eyes. She's ready for more. She knows that sex has nothing to do with us being together.

It's time.

Time for me to make love to her. Love is the optimal word here. She's my entire world, and she doesn't know it. At least not from my words. I hope that my actions tell her everything that my words can't. I know there is something that is holding her back. Something that keeps her from going all in, and until I identify what that is, I won't tell her.

I know me, and I recognize that not seeing that same love in her eyes, hearing those words echo back to me, will kill me. She's

everything I've ever wanted and never thought I would be lucky enough to have.

She has all of me.

Glancing down at my wrist, I forgot that I had taken my watch off when I came home and changed. I turn to look at the clock on the wall and see that she's ten minutes late. Walking into the kitchen, where my phone is on the island, I pick it up to call her to make sure she's all right, as Charlotte is always on time. There's a knock at the door.

Keeping my phone in my hand, I rush to the door and pull it open.

"Hey." My sexy girl waves and smiles.

"Why are you knocking on the door?" I ask.

She steps in close and wraps her arms around me while we stand here in the doorway. "I don't know," she finally says.

"Come in." She keeps her arm around my waist as we walk inside. "Did you bring an overnight bag?" For what I have planned, she's not leaving.

"Yeah, it's in the—" She stops when she realizes that the lights are down low. Soft music is playing in the background, and the dining room table is set for two, with candlelight setting the mood.

"What is all of this?" She turns to me, looking for an explanation.

"I wanted to take you out to dinner, but I also didn't want to share you."

"You sleep next to me every night," she reminds me.

"It's not enough."

"Is this some kind of scheme to convince me to move in with you?" she asks, teasing in her tone.

"No. You know I want you here. Or if not here, that we have the same address, wherever that might be. My place, yours, or somewhere new." I pull her into my chest, locking my arms around her waist. "I know that when you're ready for that, you'll let me know."

"So, that's all I have to do? Tell you I want something, and you make it happen?"

"Yes."

"You didn't even hesitate." She's grinning, and I vow to always make her smile like this.

"I'll always try like hell to give you everything you could ever want."

"I think I should try this theory." Her hands that are resting on my chest move to lock behind my neck. "I wonder what I could ask for?" She kisses me under my chin.

"While you're deciding, how about you let me feed you?"

"You cooked?"

"No. But I did bake one of those premade lasagnas and put together a salad, and I managed not to burn the garlic bread."

She chuckles, and the sound fills not only my home but my heart with love for this incredible woman. "Next time we'll make homemade lasagna together."

"It's not going to be as good as yours, but you didn't have to cook it," I tell her, making her laugh again.

"It smells so good. I didn't realize I was hungry until you started talking about it."

"Come on, Charlie girl. Let me feed you." I lead her to the dining room and pull out her chair. "I'll be right back."

"Can I help?"

I lean over the back of the chair and kiss the top of her head. "You can sit there and look beautiful while I make our plates." I step back before I get carried away, and move to dish out the food. My house, much like hers, has an open concept, so she can still see me from where she's sitting at the table.

"You know a girl could get used to this," she says.

I stop what I'm doing and look at her across the room. "Good." I hold her gaze until her cheeks turn pink and she looks away. I go back to dishing up. It takes me a few trips to drop off our plates of lasagna and salad, the garlic bread, and our drinks. Two tall glasses of lemonade follow, because I want us to have our wits about us tonight. I am not missing a moment of what I have planned for us.

During dinner, there is very little conversation. We both scarf down our meals, and I think it has something to do with the desire in the air. The chemistry between the two of us is so thick you could cut it with a knife. She senses something is up. She's being quiet, waiting for me to tell her what's next.

She wants me, and it's harder than I thought it would be to sit here at this table with her, watching her eat, when all I can do is think about making love to her for the first time. I've taken my time. I wanted her to know this wasn't just some fling for me. I wanted her to feel my need for her before we took that final step.

It's not been without difficulty to hold out. My tongue has traced every inch of her creamy soft skin, and my fingertips ache to feel her softness and her taste. She tastes like mine, but tonight we're going to be one. Connected in a way we've never been before. I've imagined it so many times over the years.

In a way, I'm glad that it took us until now to get together. Sure, I curse the time we lost, but I don't know that I would have been ready for her. I'd like to think that I would have realized the treasure she is, but I can't be certain. I mean, I thought she was stuck up and assumed she thought she was better than everyone else.

I couldn't have been more wrong.

She was mourning a profound loss, and I was the dumbass who couldn't see that it was pain, not indifference. So, yeah, tonight, it's a night that's ten years in the making, but we're finally both ready. I'm ready to be hers in every way she can think of, and my hope is that she feels the same.

"I'm so full," Charlotte says, dropping her napkin to the table. "Thank you for dinner."

"You're welcome." I stand to clear the plates, and she stands to help. "I've got this. Why don't you go grab your bag and take a shower, or change, or whatever you want to do before we settle in for the night."

"I'm not really tired," she confesses.

"Not bed, baby. Just settled. We're going to relax."

She reaches and kisses me on the cheek. "That sounds perfect." She rushes back outside to collect her bag while I clean up. I hear the front door open and close, so I glance over to see her with her overnight bag on her way to my room. Seeing her in my space and seeing how comfortable she is, causes an ache inside of me. I want her here all the time. Not just here but with me. I don't care where we are as long as we are together. I'd follow her anywhere, and the idea of that no longer scares me. I'm not sure that it ever did. I was uncertain at first how this was going to go, but now I know. It's going to go with me loving her every day of forever.

She's ready.

*We're* ready.

I finish up in the kitchen, grab two bottles of water, and turn out the lights. I make sure the front door is locked before heading upstairs to bed. When I reach my bedroom, I can see the soft glow of the lamp as I push open the door. I expect to find Charlotte in the shower or changed and under the covers with the remote in her hand, looking for what we're going to watch, but that's not what I find at all.

"Charlie." Her name is a rasp from my lips as I take in the sight before me. She's lying on top of the covers in a little purple number. It's lots of lace and skimpy as fuck, and it looks incredible on her.

"You said that all I had to do was ask, right?"

I swallow hard. Little does she know I was going to give her this anyway, but we'll do it her way. At the very moment, she looks sexy as fuck, and confident in her own skin. She's no longer hiding from me. From what we are and what we will be. Something has changed. I don't know what it is, but I'm grateful.

She's all in.

"That's right," I finally answer.

"I want you. I want all of you, Spencer. I don't want a watered-down version of what you think I want. I want you. I want us."

"Okay."

A slow, sexy smile brightens her big blue eyes. "If I would have known it would be this easy, I would have asked weeks ago."

"You weren't ready to ask weeks ago," I tell her as I strip out of my shirt, tossing it across the room to the dirty clothes basket.

"I'm ready now."

To show me her words have a double meaning, she spreads her legs and trails her hand over her belly. The sheer purple fabric is a dark contrast to her creamy skin. My eyes follow her every move as she slips her hand beneath the tiny scrap of lace that's supposed to serve as panties.

"So ready," she breathes.

That spurs me into action. I make quick work of shedding my lounge pants that I changed into when I got home and my boxer briefs. I grip my cock and squeeze tightly. I send up a silent prayer that I don't embarrass myself. She's my every fantasy.

"Tell me what you want, Charlie."

"You, Spencer."

"You have me."

"You know what I mean." She's right. I do know what she means, but I need to hear her say it. I need the words to be spoken out loud from her pouty lips.

"I need the words, baby."

"I want to feel you inside me."

*Not good enough, beautiful.* I take a step toward the bed, my cock still fisted in my hand as I make lazy strokes. "My tongue? My fingers? My cock? We have so many options. I want to make sure I give you exactly what you want."

"All of the above." She huffs out a frustrated laugh.

"Tell me."

Her heated blue eyes blazing with need settle on me. I know when she opens her mouth, it's going to be all I can do not to come from her saying the words. "I want your tongue. I want your fingers. I want your cock. I want you to fuck me. I want all of it, Spencer. All of you. Please," she adds sweetly as she licks her lips.

"Good girl," I rasp as I take my final step toward the bed, reach into the nightstand, and grab the unopened box of condoms I put there earlier today. Another fail-safe to make sure we had to wait was having no protection in the house. We've had the talk about our histories, but until I know for certain she's mine for a lifetime, I can't go bare. She'll ruin me.

"Didn't peg you as a boy scout," she teases.

"Always protecting you," I reply, and those blazing baby blues turn soft. Climbing on the bed, I settle beside her, propping my head up with one elbow while the other starts to explore. "This purple, it looks good on you."

"I hoped you would like it," she replies, her voice soft.

"I do, but I'd prefer you in nothing."

"Let me take care of that." Before I can stop her, she's rolling to the other side of the bed and standing. She quickly loses the purple nightie and the strip of lace that is supposed to be panties and crawls back on the bed on her hands and knees.

"Change of plans," she says, pushing on my shoulder so that I'll fall to my back. "I need you."

"You have me," I tell her.

"I don't see your cock inside me," she says, reaching out and gripping my cock. She makes a few long strokes before she speaks again. "I don't feel your tongue or your fingers inside me either."

"I was getting there." I smile up at her.

"Well, I think I'm going to take another ask."

"Anything."

Instead of voicing what she wants, she straddles my hips. She's still gripping my cock, lazily stroking me as if we have all night, and we do, but I don't know—no, I do know that I'm not going to last that long.

"Tell me."

"I'm ready for you."

"You think so?" I move my hand between us, and yeah, she's ready.

"Told you." She smirks.

"You're supposed to let me worship you, Charlie. Let me lavish this pussy," I say softly, tracing her clit with my thumb.

"But I'm ready now."

"You want my cock?"

"You know I do. You've been teasing me for months. You've been worshipping me for months. It's time for the main event."

She's right. Reaching beside me, I grab the unopened box of condoms and tear it open. I pull out a foil packet and hand it to her. She grins, rips open the pack, and sheaths me in a matter of seconds.

I don't take my eyes off her as she lifts up on her knees and guides me inside her. Slowly, painfully so, she lowers onto me. Her head is tilted back, and all that gorgeous auburn hair hangs loosely over her shoulders. Her eyes are closed, so I can't see her blue eyes sparkle, but I can hear her soft whimpers. I can feel her all around me.

She moans. It's a deep, throaty sound of pleasure that has my cock twitching at the same time her pussy pulses around me. She's tight as fuck, and I'm barely hanging on, and neither one of us has made a move other than burying my cock deep inside her.

She rocks her hips, and we both groan at the sensation. "It's not going to take much for me," she confesses.

"Good. Tell me what you need."

Her blue eyes open, and she smiles down at me. "I've got this." She lifts up on her knees and slams back down. I reach out and grip her hips, helping her with her next round, and we set a steady pace. I'm doing everything I can to hold off my release.

"Spencer, don't stop. Yes. Yes. Yes." She bounces on my cock like she's been there before. Like she owns it, and I guess she does.

I'm barely holding on. My hands fall from her hips, but she's not a fan of that. "No." She continues to ride me. "I need your hands. Grip me, Spencer."

I put my hands back on her hips, and lift her, pulling her down a little faster. A little harder. "I'm about to come," I tell her. "I need you there. I'm not coming before you do."

"So close," she pants.

This time when I bring her back down, I raise my hips, and she screams out my name. Her pussy squeezes my cock like a vise, and it's game over. I release everything I have inside her while she pulses around me. Her fingers dig into the skin of my chest, but I welcome the pain from her nails. It reminds me that this is real. That I just made love to her, and it was the best sex of my life, hands down.

"You were made for me," I tell her as she falls forward, resting her head on my chest while my cock is still buried inside her.

"Maybe I was," she mumbles.

"Let's get you cleaned up."

"Too tired."

I kiss the top of her head and gently move her to lie next to me on the bed.

"I need to take care of the condom, and I'll be back."

"Hurry, I might miss you," she garbles sleepily.

"That's the sex high talking," I tease. She mumbles a reply, but I don't make out what she says. Rushing to the bathroom, I take care of the condom and clean up. I'm walking out to hit the light when I see that Charlotte is still in the same spot, her hand over her eyes. Reaching into the cabinet, I wet a washcloth with warm water and turn off the light. When I reach her, I sit on the edge of the bed.

"Charlie, let me help you get cleaned up."

"Too tired," she whines, making me chuckle.

"Spread your legs for me, baby." She slowly does as I ask, and I clean her up as best as I can before tossing the washcloth into the basket, turning off the bedside lamp, and sliding into the bed beside her. I pull her into my arms, and she snuggles into me.

"Worth the wait, Spence," she mumbles, and my chest shakes with silent laughter.

I kiss the top of her head and fall asleep with my heart full of love for this woman and a smile on my face. Not because I was finally inside her but because she makes me happy.

THE *Kissing* GAMES

# Chapter
# TWENTY ONE

## Charlotte

I DIDN'T TELL HIM. I know it was wrong, and I was at his place the entire weekend. We were wrapped up in this romantic bubble, and it couldn't have been more perfect. I didn't want to ruin it. I don't know how he's going to react. What if he ends things? Sure, that might be extreme, but I don't know how things are going to go, and if that's the ending for us, I wanted our weekend. I wanted to stay in that bubble of love we had created. We haven't said the words yet, but I love him.

I love him more today than I did yesterday, and I know for certain I'll love him more tomorrow. I needed it this weekend. I wanted those memories to hold on to just in case my omission tears us apart. The worst thing is, I'm overthinking this. I know I am. It's what I do, but that fear lingers inside me anyway. He only wants the best for me, and me getting the equivalent of a promotion is an incredible thing, but still, I also don't want to offend him.

What if he thinks I'm leaving because of him? Or because I don't like his company? I sigh, annoyed because I keep talking myself around in circles, and I know the only way to deal with this is by being honest. It's what I want from our relationship, and I need to make it right.

That's why it's Monday morning, and I'm walking into Dr. Phillips's office to hand him one of the two resignation letters I just printed. I should have told Spencer before him, but I know Spencer has a full day of meetings, so the chance of Dr. Phillips talking to him before I can tonight when we get home—well, to his place—is slim.

"Knock, knock," I say, doing the act on the door frame at the same time.

"Charlotte, good morning. Come on in." He waves me in. "How was your weekend?"

"Really good." I smile, and it's genuine. It was the best weekend I've ever had. "I have something for you." I rush to say the words, handing him the folded sheet of paper. I wipe my hands on my dress pants as I watch him read it. I don't technically have to give him notice since we are now hospital-owned, but Dr. Phillips hired me right out of college, and out of respect for him and the opportunity he's given me, I printed a copy of my letter for him as well.

Once he's finished, he lowers the paper to his desk and takes his reading glasses off, placing them on his desk. "Is there anything I can do to make you change your mind?"

"No." I shake my head. "This is an incredible opportunity for me. One I've always wanted."

He nods. I told him this very thing when he interviewed me for this position. "I always knew you would leave us, but I had hoped." He clears his throat. "Does this have anything to do with the buyout?"

"It gave me the push that I needed to see if my dream position was out there, and I was lucky enough to find it not far from home."

"Well, I guess congratulations are in order. You'll keep in touch, right? Stop by and see us from time to time. We're really going to miss you around here. You've implemented processes and procedures that have this place running better than it has in years."

I smile at him. "Thank you. I'm just a phone call away if you need anything."

"You're going to be hard to replace."

"I'm happy to help with interviews in the evenings if you need me to. I can help out in the evenings and on weekends, whatever you need until you fill the role."

"Thank you, Charlotte. Your offer just confirms the class act that you are. I'll try not to bother you. We have a bigger support system now, and we'll let them handle it. You go off and be great like we know you will be at your new job. I wish you nothing but the best."

My eyes well up with tears. "Thank you so much. Thank you for the opportunity to work here and for giving me a chance right out of college. I will never forget my time here."

"We were lucky to have you, Charlotte. You're good at what you do, and I'm certain you'll excel at your new position."

I nod and stand, knowing I'm seconds away from losing control of my tears. Dr. Phillips nods as I give him a watery smile and walk out of his office. I manage not to run into any of the other staff members on the way to my office. I already have an email drafted that I plan to send out at the end of the day, letting them know that I'm leaving. I don't want to risk one of them somehow getting word back to Spencer before I get a chance to tell him.

Sitting behind my desk, I make sure the other letter is in my purse, and I get to work. I have a lot to do in the next two weeks to make sure everyone knows where I am on projects and processes that are in place. I plan to type up as much as I can to make this transition easy for the next person.

I glance at the clock, and it's just after eight. Spencer and I made plans to stay at his place again tonight, and that's fine with me. My house no longer feels like home to me. He does, but maybe it's he who makes me feel that way. Shaking out of my thoughts, I get to work. I have a lot to do.

THE *Kissing* GAMES

As soon as I walk through the door, I kick off my heels. I need to change and pack a bag for Spencer's. I told him I'd be there at six. I'm picking up dinner that I've already called in on my way, so I need to get moving. I have my pants unbuttoned and halfway down my thighs when I hear a knock at the front door. I have no idea who it could be, but I can't answer the door without pants. I pull them back up and work on fastening the button as I walk to the front door.

I don't have time for visitors. I'm antsy and nervous as hell about how Spencer is going to react, and I just need to get to him. I need to see him and spill my secret and hope like hell I'm still going to be sleeping in his arms tonight.

I pull open the door and gasp. "Spence. Hi. I thought we were meeting at your place?" He just stares at me for a few minutes. His hair is disheveled as if he's been running his hands through it. His suit jacket has been discarded, and the sleeves of his black button-up is rolled up to his elbows, showing off his tattoos. He looks sexy as hell, but I can't think about that right now.

He doesn't speak, so I step back and motion for him to enter as I tell him to do so. "Come in." He walks inside, and I shut the door. I'm nervous, and I know that it will show, so I move to the couch and sit, pulling a pillow onto my lap to hold against me to hopefully keep me from fidgeting.

Spencer surprises me when he falls to his knees in front of me, taking my hands with his. His chocolate eyes are filled with an emotion I can't name. I've never seen him like this before, and it's scaring me. Did something happen? Is someone hurt? My mind races with what could have him in this state.

My hand trembles with fear for what he's about to tell me as I rest it against his cheek. He places his hand over mine and closes his eyes. When they finally open, it's determination that I see.

"Spencer—" I start, but he shakes his head.

"I love you. I'm in love with you."

My heart stalls and then starts again for him. The rapid rhythm beating in my chest is just for him. Guilt weighs on me, but he's lost in his thoughts. I'll let him talk, and then I'll tell him. I can't wait. I need to tell him that I love him too, but not before he knows what I've been hiding from him. It's not a huge secret, but a secret

THE *Kissing* GAMES

all the same. There are no secrets in relationships, and I know I'm going to have to work hard to prove to him that he can trust me. I'll never stop every day. As long as he stays with me, I'll fight to show him I'll never keep anything from him ever again.

"I think I loved you then, you know? I saw you across the auditorium, and I knew. I just knew that I needed to know you. Over the years, I've thought about you often. When Audrey started dating Linc, I was stoked that I'd still get to see you." He laughs as he laces his fingers with mine.

"I can't lose you, Charlie. I won't lose you. So wherever you're going, I'm going too. We'll figure it out, but I won't let you go. Now that I have you. Fuck, this past weekend, that's what our life will be like. I'll cherish you every day of forever, just... let me come with you."

"What are you talking about?" I ask softly. My heart still hammers in my chest, but on the outside, I'm calm, cool, and collected.

"Lucia, she told me you're leaving, and I'm going with you." There is strong determination in his voice. "I've finally got you, and I can't let go, Charlie. Please don't make me let go." He moves in close and places his hands on my cheeks. "I am in love with you. You are the love of my life, and I'd follow you anywhere."

I'm struggling to keep up with what's going on or what he thinks is going on, but then I realize Lucia must have found out I'm leaving. She ran to him and told him so, but it's all twisted, and it's my fault. The sadness in his eyes is my fault.

"I'm not going anywhere."

His brows furrow. "Lucia said you turned in your notice, that you found a new job and you're leaving town. I don't have grounds to fire her, even though I wish I did, but I'll quit. I'm going to give notice in the morning, and I'll go with you." He leans in and presses his lips to the corner of my mouth, and I have to choke back a sob.

"Come here." I motion for him to sit next to me on the couch, and he does, pulling me into his arms. He locks them tightly around me, and I let him hold me while I try to find the words to fix this mess. I know that I need to see him. I need to look him in the eye, so he can see my truths. So I move to straddle him. He wraps his arms around me, locking his hands behind my back, holding me tightly.

"I don't know how she found out, but I did put in my notice today. I found a new job, but, Spence, I'm not leaving town. It's in Calloway." His brow furrows, so I continue to try and unravel this mess that I've made with Lucia's meddling. "When I found out that you were going to be my new boss, I started looking. In the beginning, it was because I couldn't stand the thought of working under you." His shoulders sag, but I rush to get the rest out. "However, that was before we were us." I run my fingers through his hair. "I was still looking, but it was because I didn't want to be the woman who slept her way to the top. I wanted us to be partners, and working beneath you, even if not directly, made that part of our relationship feel unbalanced. You know that I was uncomfortable with you being my boss, even if not directly. However, it was more than that. This job, it's what I've always wanted. I knew that my position at the pediatric office was temporary. It was a stepping stone of sorts, but I got comfortable and complacent. When I applied for this job, there was a little bit of Spencer won't be my boss, and we could be free to be together without worry or concern, at least on my end, and a whole lot of this is what I want."

"You're not leaving?"

"No. I'm quitting my job. I told Dr. Phillips this morning. He must have reached out to Lucia. I accepted a new position at Calloway Cancer Center. I'm their new COO."

"Baby." He swallows hard. "I'm so fucking happy for you and even happier for me. That bitch, she told me you were quitting and moving away."

"I'm sorry I kept this from you. It wasn't that I didn't want to tell you. Every interview and every phone call of the process, I wanted to discuss it with you. I just... I wanted to get this job on my own merit. I didn't want you to make a phone call on my behalf." He smirks, and I point at him. "See! I wanted to do this on my own. I wanted them to want me for me, not because the CEO of Charleston's hospital and my boyfriend called to put a good word in for me."

He slides one hand behind my neck and pulls me in close. "I don't want there to be secrets between us. You are my best friend, my lover, and my future. I would have listened if you told me not to interfere."

"So, you admit you would have."

He grins. "I already told you, anything you want, if it's within my power, I'll give it to you."

"I love you."

His eyes soften hearing my words. "I love you too."

"Are we okay?"

"We are more than okay. I came here thinking you were leaving me, and find out you're not."

"We don't have to worry about anyone talking when they see us together now," I tell him with a smile.

"I didn't worry before, but I'm glad this sets your mind at ease. I'm happy that you found your dream job, and I'm even happier that you're here, you're staying, and you're mine."

He kisses me softly and sweetly, and for the first time in months, I can breathe easily. When I pull back from his lips, his hand falls to my lap, and I wrap my arms around him in a hug. I close my eyes and take in the moment. There is nothing holding me back. I realize my fears were my insecurities, but he loves me. I love him, and I want a life with him.

I'm ready.

I want him.

I want us.

"I have one more secret," I tell him.

"Let's hear it, baby."

"You were never a four, or even a five. That first kiss at the resort? A ten. Hands down."

"Come here, you." He presses his lips to mine and proves his ten status. My heart thumps in my chest just thinking of us starting our lives together. Nothing between us but the love that we share. No secrets. No worries. Just love.

That's when an idea hits me. "You know, maybe I should think about moving. Calloway is about thirty-five minutes from my place."

He knows me so well. "Yeah, you know, if you decide you need to live closer, my place is only thirty minutes from Calloway," he offers.

"Are you asking me to move in with you?" I laugh.

"I'm asking you to be mine. If that means you're ready to live with me, then yes. Hell fucking yes, I want you to live with me. We're forever, Charlie girl. I want that sooner than later, but I'll be patient. I've been on this forever trail a lot longer than you have."

"I think that it's time the train stops to pick me up."

His eyes darken, but there's still a sparkle in them. "Now? Tonight?"

I chuckle. "Is that what you want?"

"Yes."

"Okay. Then we can start tonight."

He stands with me wrapped around him, and I squeal as he carries me down the hall to my room. "What are you doing?" I laugh.

"Making love to you here for the last time." He tosses me on the bed.

"I have an entire house to pack up."

"Yeah, but you won't be calling it home. No more your place or mine. It's ours. If you don't like the house, we'll sell it and buy or build, or whatever. I don't care as long as you come home to me every night."

"I love your house," I tell him honestly. "I like your idea of raising a family there." I hold his gaze as he smiles down at me. All it took was hearing him tell me that he loves me, and I'm already talking babies.

"When?"

"When what?" I ask, even though I know what he's asking.

"Babies, Charlie girl. When are you going to give me babies?"

My heart melts. "One step at a time, Spence."

"You're really moving in with me?" he asks as he begins to strip out of his clothes.

"I'm really moving in with you."

"I need you naked, baby." He grins when I scramble off the bed to do his bidding.

THE *Kissing* GAMES

Once I'm stripped out of my clothes, I climb back on the bed, and he follows after me. He kisses me soundly before pulling back and cursing. "Fuck."

"What's wrong?"

"I don't have a condom."

I lock my legs behind his back. "We don't need them. I'm on the pill, and we've already talked about our histories."

"You can stop taking it," he tells me.

I smile up at my sweet, sexy man. "I will in time. Right now, I need you inside me."

"Anything," he says as he slides deep. He stills and rests his forehead against mine. "Nothing has ever felt like this before. Feeling you without anything between us— It's... fuck me, baby. This is heaven. I love you. I love you so much."

"I love you too."

He kisses me again as he starts to move, and it's not lost on me that I'm going to spend the rest of my life kissing my rival.

THE *Kissing* GAMES

# Epilogue

## Charlotte

### *Six months later*

I'M STARING DOWN AT MY engagement ring, something I've done a lot of the last week since Spencer proposed. I've been thinking a lot about what I might have in mind for my wedding, and I don't need all the fanfare. I just want to be his wife. I don't desire a big wedding, or hell, a wedding at all for that matter. We could go to the courthouse, and I'd be more than fine with it. However, I'm going to need to convince my fiancé that's what I want.

I just want him and the life that we're building. I don't require more than that. Just Spencer.

"Do you not like it?" he asks, walking into the bedroom. It's Sunday night, and we're getting ready for bed.

"I love it. I was just thinking about our wedding."

"Anything you want, Charlie girl," he assures me.

"I've been thinking about it a lot, and I don't really want a wedding."

"You don't?" he asks.

"No. I just want to be your wife, Spencer."

He nods and grabs his cell phone from the nightstand. His fingers tap at the screen before the phone rings. I'm curious, but I don't ask. When I hear his mom answer, I'm surprised and even more intrigued.

"Hey, kid," she greets.

"Hi, Mom."

"Everything okay?"

"Yes. Everything is fine. Charlie and I were just talking about the wedding."

"Oh. What can I do?"

"Well, we were thinking of something intimate. Maybe even just the two of us."

"And you're asking for my permission?"

"Not your permission but your thoughts?"

She chuckles. "Spencer, weddings are for the guests, but the sentiment is for those pledging to share their lives together. You know that your father and I eloped, and I don't regret it, not for a single second."

"So, you wouldn't be mad if you missed it?"

"No, son, and neither would your father. We know how much you love her, and we also know this has to be hard for her. She doesn't have her parents, and that, well, that has to be tough. We support you no matter what. In fact, I encourage it. I'm hopeful that means I'll be getting grandbabies to spoil soon." You can hear the love and the happiness in her voice for us. My own happiness and love has tears springing to my eyes. His parents have accepted me with open arms, and I love them as much as I love their son.

"Thanks, Mom. I love you." He winks at me. "I need to go now. It's time I convince my fiancée that we need to start making babies."

"Spencer!" I scold, then smack my hand over my mouth, and his mom laughs.

THE *Kissing* GAMES

"Hi, Charlie," she says through the phone.

"Hi."

"Gotta go. Tell Dad we said hello, and we'll be in touch." Spencer ends the call.

"Love you both," she says, and tears fill my eyes.

"I knew that's what she would say, but I also know you. I know that you would have worried about how they would feel. I need you to hear it from her unprompted. You tell me when, and you tell me where, and I'm all in, baby."

I process what his mom said, and I think about my sister and my life with Spencer, and I don't want to wait another day to be his wife. "The courthouse works, and then we can have a get-together here."

"How about we go away and do a destination wedding? Just the two of us. Combine that with our honeymoon, maybe work on our first baby while we're there, and then we celebrate with everyone when we get home?"

"Yes." My voice cracks. My answer is simple and instant. Hot tears prick my eyes, but they never fall. "I don't care where or when, but soon would be good."

"Wait? Are you letting me handle it?" he asks.

I nod. "I am. I can get the time off work. Susan already told me when she saw the ring."

He moves off the bed and grabs his laptop from the nightstand, and within the hour, we have a room, flights, and a destination wedding booked in the Bahamas. "Two weeks," he says, putting his laptop back on the nightstand. "Two weeks and you're my wife."

"I'm ready," I assure him. I'm a little sad that Audrey won't be there, but at the same time, I know she'll understand. I have never been a "big wedding" kind of girl, and definitely not after losing our parents. At the end of the day, all that matters is that I get to spend the rest of my life with the man I love. Audrey will be happy for us. I know she will.

"I'm so fucking ready," he says, holding me tighter as we drift off to sleep.

THE *Kissing* GAMES

# *Epilogue*

## *Spencer*

### *One year later*

FOR TWO DAYS, I'VE SLEPT on this uncomfortable chair-bed thing that the hospital provides. I've already told Cheryl to find me some vendors for something more comfortable. Dads need to be comfortable too.

Regardless of my sleeping conditions, I'm a happy man. How could I not be when I'm holding my son in my arms? Emmett Spencer Pennington came into the world two days ago via a cesarian section. He and his momma are doing well, and my heart, it's so full, I feel as if my chest might explode.

"Daddy loves you," I tell him softly, trying not to wake my wife.

"I love seeing you with him," Charlie's sleepy voice greets me.

I smile at her, and the emotions that have been overtaking me the past couple of days threaten to choke me. I swallow them back and stand, carrying Emmett and handing him off to his momma.

I sit next to them on the bed and wrap my arms around both of them.

My family.

My entire heart.

"Thank you, Charlie. For loving me, for giving me this life, this little man. I don't have the words." I clear my throat.

"You never gave up on me." She smiles up at me before turning her gaze back to our son.

"I think he needs a little brother and definitely a little sister," I tell her, to take some of the heavy out of the room.

"Maybe you can let her heal from this one, son." I hear from the doorway, and I look up to see my parents.

"How are you feeling, Charlie?" Mom asks as she comes to stand next to her on the other side of the bed.

"Sore but blessed."

Mom leans over and kisses her cheek. "I hear you're getting out of here today?"

"That's the plan," Charlie answers.

"Well, we've just dropped off a week's worth of meals to your freezer." Dad chuckles. "And your mom placed an overnight bag for both of us in one of the spare bedrooms. We're ready to give you a break when you need it."

I look down at my wife to find tears rolling down her cheeks. "Thank you," she says softly. "We're going to need you. Our family needs you," she tells them.

"Oh, sweetheart." Mom places her hand on her arm. "I know we can't replace them, but we will make sure to shower you with so much love, you'll feel them with you every day."

Charlie nods, and I have to swallow back my own emotions. I would give anything for her parents to be here with us.

"Do you want to hold him?" Charlie asks my mom.

"Papaw gets dibs this time. Grandma hogged him yesterday." My dad gently moves Mom out of the way and takes Emmett into his arms. "Now, let's talk about all the fun we're going to have." He moves to the end of the bed where chairs are placed, and Mom follows after him, not willing to miss a moment with her new grandson.

"I guess we need to have at least one more to even out the odds." Charlie laughs.

"We can add on," I tell her, and her laughter fills the room and my heart.

Who would have thought that a kissing game with my rival would have made my heart this full? Leaning over, I place a kiss on her temple as we watch my parents fawn over our son. I wish I'd known then what I know now, and I would have fought harder for her. It just wasn't our time, but here and now, it's us. It's our son, and it's our forever.

# Thank YOU

for reading *Kissing the Rival*.

Want more of the Kissing Games Series?

**Kissing My Brother's Bride**
Molly McLain

**Kissing the Rival**
Kaylee Ryan

**Kissing My Crush**
C.A. Harms

**Kissing A Stranger**
Lacey Black

**Kissing My Soulmate**
Evan Grace

THE *Kissing* GAMES

# Contact
## KAYLEE RYAN

**Facebook:**
bit.ly/2C5DgdF

**Reader Group:**
bit.ly/2o0yWDx

**Goodreads:**
bit.ly/2HodJvx

**BookBub:**
bit.ly/2KulVvH

**Website:**
kayleeryan.com/

# More from KAYLEE RYAN

### *With You Series:*
Anywhere with You | More with You | Everything with You

### *Soul Serenade Series:*
Emphatic | Assured | Definite | Insistent

### *Southern Heart Series:*
Southern Pleasure | Southern Desire
Southern Attraction | Southern Devotion

### *Unexpected Arrivals Series*
Unexpected Reality |Unexpected Fight | Unexpected Fall
Unexpected Bond | Unexpected Odds

### *Riggins Brothers Series:*
Play by Play | Layer by Layer | Piece by Piece
Kiss by Kiss | Touch by Touch | Beat by Beat

### *Entangled Hearts Duet:*
Agony | Bliss

### *Cocky Hero Club:*
Lucky Bastard

### *Mason Creek Series:*
Perfect Embrace

THE *Kissing* GAMES

# More from KAYLEE RYAN

### *Standalone Titles:*
Tempting Tatum | Unwrapping Tatum
Levitate | Just Say When
I Just Want You | Reminding Avery

Hey, Whiskey | Pull You Through | Remedy
The Difference | Trust the Push | Forever After All
Misconception | Never with Me

### *Out of Reach Series:*
Beyond the Bases | Beyond the Game
Beyond the Play | Beyond the Team

## Co-written with Lacey Black:

### *Fair Lakes Series:*
It's Not Over | Just Getting Started | Can't Fight It

### *Standalone Titles:*
Boy Trouble | Home to You | Beneath the Fallen Stars

### *Co-writing as Rebel Shaw with Lacey Black:*
Royal | Crying Shame

THE *Kissing* GAMES

# Acknowledgments

*To my readers:*

Thank you for continuing to show your support with reading each and every release. I cannot tell you what that means to me. Thank you for taking the journey with me.

*To my family:*

I love you. You hold me up and support me every day. I can't imagine my life without you as my support system. Thank you for believing in me, and being there to celebrate my success.

*Wander Aguiar:*

Thank you for another amazing image.

*Tami Integrity Formatting:*

Thank you for making Kissing the Rival beautiful. You're amazing and I cannot thank you enough for all that you do.

*The Book Cover Boutique:*

You nailed the covers for this series. Never a doubt, my friend.

*My beta team:*

Jamie, Stacy, Lauren, Erica, and Franci I would be lost without you. You read my words as much as I do, and I can't tell you what your input and all the time you give means to me. Countless messages and bouncing ideas, you ladies keep me sane with the characters are being anything but. Thank you from the bottom of my heart for taking this wild ride with me.

*My ARC Team:*

An amazing group of readers who shout about my books from the rooftops, and I couldn't be more grateful for every single one of you. Thank you for being a part of the team, and a critical part of every single release.

*Give Me Books:*

With every release, your team works diligently to get my book in the hands of bloggers. I cannot tell you how thankful I am for your services.

*Grey's Promotions:*

Thank you for your support with this release. I am so grateful for your team.

*Deaton Author Services, Jo Thompson, & Jess Hodge:*

Thank you for giving this book a fresh set of eyes. I appreciate each of you helping me make this book the best that it can be.

*Becky Johnson:*

I could not do this without you. Thank you for pushing me, and making me work for it.

*Chasidy Renee:*

You're a rockstar. Thank you for all that you do.

*Molly McLain:*

Thank you for asking me to be a part of this project.

*Lacey Black:*

There isn't much I can say that I have not already, except for I love ya, girl. Your friendship means the world to me. Thank you for being you.

*Bloggers:*

Thank you doesn't seem like enough. You don't get paid to do what you do. It's from the kindness of your heart and your love of reading that fuels you. Without you, without your pages, your voice, your reviews, spreading the word it would be so much harder, if not impossible, to get my words in reader's hands. I can't tell you how much your never-ending support means to me. Thank you for being you, thank you for all that you do.

*To my Kaylee's Crew Members:*

You are my people. I love chatting with you. I'm honored to have you on this journey with me. Thank you for reading, sharing, commenting, suggesting, the teasers, the messages all of it. Thank you from the bottom of my heart for all that you do. Your support is everything!

Much love,

*Kaylee Ryan*
AUTHOR

Printed in Great Britain
by Amazon

23691688R00130